A Note from the Author

I would like to extend my gratitude to Edgar Rice Burroughs, Inc., for their kindness in allowing me to introduce Dawn and Bunduki, adoptive great-granddaughter and adopted son of Lord Greystoke, TARZAN OF THE APES.

I would also like to thank Philip José Farmer, whose book *TARZAN ALIVE* supplied much useful information and details of the Greystoke family's lineage. Also Fred Bear of Grayling, Michigan, Ben Pearson of Pine Bluff, Arkansas, and William D. Randall of Orlando, Florida (listed alphabetically) for supplying my heroine's and hero's bows, arrows and knives. I wanted them to have the best.

—J. T. Edson

BUNDUKI

J. T. Edson

DAW BOOKS, INC.

DONALD A. WOLLHEIM, PUBLISHER

1301 Avenue of the Americas
New York, N. Y.   10019

FIRST PRINTING, JULY 1976

1 2 3 4 5 6 7 8 9

PRINTED IN U.S.A.

This book is dedicated to the
memory of the world's greatest
action-escapism-adventure writer:—
EDGAR RICE BURROUGHS

CHAPTER ONE

Where Is Dawn?

THE screaming of monkeys aroused James Allenvale Gunn, better known throughout Europe, Africa, Asia, North and South America and Australia as "Bunduki" —the Swahili word which means a firearm of any kind —as he lay on a crotch formed by the junction of two thick branches. Like a wild animal, or a man who had lived long under dangerous conditions, he came from the depths of sleep to instant and complete awakefulness without any dull-witted, fumbling transitory period. With an agile movement, he rose to his feet. Balancing himself instinctively, he looked around him so as to find out what, if anything, had disturbed the monkeys.

Suddenly, a realization of what he was seeing flooded through him!

It was followed by amazement and disbelief!

Shaking his head, as if to try and clear it, he discovered that his first impressions were unchanged.

He really *was* standing high in a tree, surrounded by what was obviously a tropical jungle!

Surely his eyes must be playing tricks upon him?

Even as that thought came, it was replaced by other and more alarming questions!

Where was the Land Rover, with old M'Bili slumped dead over the steering-wheel, the struggling, terror-striken impala ram and the sheer walls of the Gambuti Gorge into which they had all been tumbling?

And, infinitely more important, where could Dawn be?

Bunduki recollected with frightening clarity that his adoptive cousin had been with him, helping to restrain the impala, when their vehicle had toppled over the edge of the Gorge to what ought to have been certain destruction.

Yet Dawn was nowhere in sight!

Only the leaves, branches, creepers, trees and undergrowth of the jungle met his searching eyes.

There was, as Bunduki had good cause to know, no such jungle anywhere within five hundred miles of the Ambagasali Wild Life Reserve.

Holding his churning emotions in check with an effort of will, Bunduki took stock of his surroundings and drew certain conclusions.

According to the position of the sun, the time was early morning. That suggested a night had passed since his last conscious memory. Or it could have been longer, he had no way of knowing.

Yesterday afternoon, if that was when it had been, Dawn and Bunduki had been carrying out a routine patrol of the Reserve. It had been the normal, practically everyday task for him in his capacity as Chief Warden; except that his adoptive cousin did not often have the opportunity to accompany him. As the University of Ambagasali—at which she was a physical education instructress—was on vacation, she had taken advantage of it to spend a few days with him. Accompanied by the Head Ranger, M'Bili, they had been checking on the condition of the animals and searching for evidence that poachers had been at work.

Circling vultures had guided them to where an impala ram was struggling in the clutch of a wire snare. Its body had been cut badly, but they had felt that it could be healed. So they had freed it and carried it to the vehicle.

Fate had started to weave its web from that moment!

When loading the Land Rover that morning, M'Bili had forgotten to include the first aid bag. So they had not been carrying the means to render the frightened animal unconscious. Telling the aged Head Ranger to drive, Bunduki had ridden in the back with Dawn. It had required both their efforts and knowledge of wild creatures to control the terrified animal and prevent its struggles from inflicting further injuries upon itself. If it had not been for that, they would have been occupying the front seat.

They had been returning to Headquarters along the trail which ran parallel to the edge of the Gambuti Gorge and the charge from a shotgun had torn through the windshield of the Land Rover. The attack had probably been the work of a native poacher who had seen and identified the official vehicle and was afraid that his own presence would be detected.

Caught in the head by some of the buckshot balls, M'Bili had collapsed on to the steering-wheel. At the same time, he had inadvertantly turned the vehicle towards the Gorge and had trodden upon the accelerator. Before Bunduki or Dawn—neither of whom had been hit by the missiles—could make a move to avert the catastrophe, the speeding Land Rover had carried them over the edge.

They had been falling to their deaths!

Over three hundred feet below, the jagged rocks and raging current of the Gambuti River had been awaiting their arrival. If one failed to kill them, the other was certain to do it.

Yet, as Bunduki was still alive, it appeared that neither the rocks nor the swiftly-flowing water had done its work.

Where *was* his adoptive cousin?

"Dawn!" Bunduki bellowed, with all the power and volume he could muster. "Dawn, can you hear me?"

There was no reply!

The silence was only broken by the sudden rustling, crackling, crashing and shaking of the foliage above him as the monkeys fled.

Instinctively, Bunduki looked upwards. He hoped that he might learn something from the animals' behaviour which would help him to understand the almost inexplicable situation in which he found himself.

Using their long tails as aids to their hands and feet, the reddish-brown coloured monkeys went racing nimbly away through the foliage. Unless he missed his guess, it had been his voice and nothing else that had frightened them away.

For all that, something was wrong!

A moment's consideration informed Bunduki what it was.

No species of monkey in Africa had a prehensile tail, such a thick reddish coat, beard and body shape.

If Bunduki did not know it was impossible, he would have sworn that the departing animals were red howler monkeys.

A species found only in South America!

Staring with greater concentration, Bunduki double-checked the details of the creatures' appearances. They had not gone far, but had come to a halt in a nearby tree and were staring back with an equal curiosity. No matter how much he sought for evidence to the contrary, he found only further proof that he was correct. They were a family of *Alouatta Seviculus,* the South American red howler monkey.

Frowning in bewilderment, Bunduki raised his right hand with the intention of thrusting back his hair. It was an instinctive gesture which he always employed when perturbed or puzzled. However, on this occasion, it went unfinished.

As the hand came into his range of vision, he saw that it was covered by the ventilated pigskin glove which he always wore when hunting with his bow and arrows.

The discovery caused other sensations to register in his mind.

His feet were bare!

The slight breeze felt as if it was blowing on predominantly naked flesh!

Looking down, so as to ascertain the reason for this phenomenon, Bunduki could not prevent a startled exclamation from bursting out of his lips.

The garments which he had been wearing in the

Land Rover—a khaki bush-shirt, slacks and calf-high hunting boots—were all gone. Instead, he had on the glove, a brown leather archer's armguard strapped to his left wrist* and a loincloth made from a leopard's skin and held up by a two-and-a-quarter-inch broad leather belt. In its sheath, on the left side of the belt, hung a big knife that looked *very* familiar.

Drawing the knife, Bunduki stared in puzzlement at it. There was no doubt why he recognized it. It had been presented to him on his twenty-first birthday by his adoptive parents, Lord and Lady Greystoke. Made by the master cutler, W.D. Randall Jr., of Orlando, Florida, it was called a Model 12 "Smithsonian Bowie." Weighing forty-three ounces, it had an overall length of sixteen and a half inches. Its eleven inches long, two-and-a-quarter-inches wide, clip pointed** blade was three-eighths of an inch thick at the stock and had been modelled on the original weapon made in the 1820's by the Arkansas blacksmith, James Black, for the legendary James Bowie.

A slight movement to Bunduki's left attracted his attention. Instinctively, as he turned his head to investigate, his right hand crossed to grasp the concave ivory hilt—the lugged guard, scolloped collar and butt cap of which were made of brass—ready to draw the knife if necessary. He did not find any danger was threatening him, only the cause of yet another puzzle. Suspended from a broken branch, close above where he had been lying, were a bow and a quiver filled with arrows.

And not just *any* bow!

It was Bunduki's own, produced to his specifications by the Bear Archery Division of Grayling, Michigan. Sixty inches long, it was a black Super Kodiak with

---

*The armguard is used to protect the flesh of the inner arm from the slap of the bow's string.
**Clip point: one where the back of the blade curves to meet the cutting edge in a concave arc. In the case of Bunduki's Model 12, the "false," or top cutting edge was five and a quarter inches in length and as sharp as the main cutting edge.

fiber glass limbs which gave a draw of one hundred pounds. Attached to its right side was a bow-quiver holding eight arrows. Their buff coloured fiber glass shafts told him that each had a Bear Four-Blade Razorhead hunting point.

The same applied to the fourteen arrows in the leather back-quiver which was hanging alongside the bow. All were equipped with hunting heads. There was not one of the type he used when catching animals alive for examination. Out of curiosity, he opened the pouch on the front of the quiver. He found that it held the stone which he used for keeping exceptionally sharp edges on the points of his hunting arrows. There were also six new, double-loop, braided black Dacron bow-strings. While he always carried the stone, he could not recollect having put the spare strings in the pouch.

Nor, if it came to that, had he been carrying his archery equipment with him when he and his adoptive cousin had set off on the fateful patrol.

"Where is Dawn?"

The question returned to take precedence over all others.

Compared with the very deep concern that Bunduki was experiencing over his adoptive cousin's welfare, the strange situation in which he found himself was of minor importance.

Slowly, but inexorably, a thought began to creep into Bunduki's mind. It refused to be ignored and suggested that Dawn had been rescued in that same unexplained, practically miraculous fashion as himself. Not only that. She was somewhere to the north-west—taking the position of the sun as an aid to compass directions—alive, uninjured—but possibly in great danger!

Bunduki was at a loss to explain the reason for the feeling that he was experiencing. Certainly it was something completely outside all his previous knowledge and nothing like it had ever happened to him before. He could not shake off the compulsion to go and investigate the validity of the thought

Nor did he try to do so.

Dawn was alive and might be in peril!

Bunduki needed to know no more than that!

For the time being, nothing else mattered!

How the rescue had been performed, by whom, for what purpose—the way in which he was dressed and armed implied that it was probably for more than reasons of humanity—even where Dawn and he had been transported, all faded into unimportance.

Dawn was not dead!

So Bunduki must go and find her!

Once they were reunited, they could try to discover the answers to the questions which must be plaguing her as well as himself.

Taking down the quiver, Bunduki swung its strap over his head and settled it on his back so that the arrows would be readily accessible to his gloved hand as it reached over his right shoulder. Then he lifted the immensely powerful, recurved* hunting bow from the branch. It was already strung, which suggested that whoever had rescued him must have considerable knowledge of archery. Even a new string had been fitted. Never had the smooth, carefully contoured hardwood of the handle-riser felt so comforting as when his left thumb and forefinger enfolded it.

No matter who, or what, Bunduki's saviours proved to be, he considered that they had given him adequate means of survival in any kind of jungle that he had ever seen. It was almost as if they had known his skills and capabilities, and had supplied him with what, in his case, were the basic necessities to stay alive.

Standing on the crotch, Bunduki looked ideally suited to meet the challenge of his surroundings. Six-foot three-inches in height, he had blond hair taken straight back and a tanned, exceptionally handsome face. While his blue eyes could twinkle with merriment, they were at that moment as cold and chilling as a June sky just before a storm. He had a tremendous

---

*Recurved bow: one that is bent back from the straight line at the end of its limbs.

spread to his shoulders, with massive biceps and forearms to match. His bronzed torso slimmed down at
the waist, with the stomach ridged by cords of powerful muscles, then spread to long legs which were so
well-developed that they could carry his two hundred and twenty pounds weight with a light-footed and
effortless-seeming agility.

For all his great size and enormous strength,
Bunduki could have come close to world record class
as a sprinter, long distance runner, swimmer and gymnast. There was, however, more than sheer physical
prowess to his make-up. Most of his education and upbringing had been a superb preparation for whatever
might lie ahead.

Having learned that a gang of Mau Mau terrorists
were planning to attack their friend Major Roger
Gunn's farm, Lord Greystoke, his son, Sir Paul John
Clayton—Clayton being the Greystoke's family name
—adopted son, Sir John Drummond-Clayton and his
son, Armand John Drummond-Clayton,* had rushed
to the rescue. Unfortunately, by the time they had arrived, Major Gunn and his wife had been murdered.
Bunduki, then only three years old, had been saved
by a loyal servant. With her usual compassion, Lady
Jane Greystoke had adopted the orphan and he was
raised as one of their family.

During the years which had followed, Bunduki was
given a very thorough formal and practical education.
However, he had become disenchanted with the so-
called permissive society in England. So, instead of entering a university after he had left Eton, he had returned to Kenya. From there, he had accompanied
Lord Greystoke, Sir Paul, Sir John and Armand Drummond-Clayton on the various expeditions—which had

---

*For those who have read Addendum 3 (The Greystroke
Lineage) in fictionist genealogist Philip José Farmer's TARZAN
ALIVE, to avoid confusion, the author has transposed the
Christian names of Sir John Paul Clayton and John Armand
Drummond-Clayton.

taken them into many primitive parts of the world—
undertaken on behalf of bodies like the International
Union For Conservation and Natural Resources.

While travelling and when at home on the Greystokes' property in Kenya, even before leaving school,
Bunduki had gained a vast amount of experience in a
variety of subjects. In his hands, the Smithsonian bowie
knife was an even more effective weapon than James
Bowie had found the original to be. Armand had taught
him the techniques employed by British Commandos,
American Rangers and European resistance fighters in
World War II, but which had been unknown in Bowie's
day. With his bow and arrows he had performed
many of the feats attributed to Robin Hood. Although
his mysterious rescuers had not provided him with
either, he could handle an *assegai*—short, stabbing
spear—and shield like a Zulu warrior, or hurl a *m'kuki*
—long, throwing spear—as well as any Masai or Samburu *moran*.* His instructor, Muviro, chief of the
Waziri—who had served with members of all three nations in the Kings African Rifles and had learned their
fighting arts—had also taught him the use of a *simi*,**
battle-axe and war club. He was also well-versed in
boxing, *judo, karate* and plain, old fashioned rough-
house brawling.

From the male members of his adopted family, ex-
perts all, Bunduki had learned to read tracks that were
barely discernible to less skilled eyes. He had been
taught how to move as silently as any great cat, even
through thick undergrowth. He also knew much about
animals; how to hunt them for food when necessary,
or how to avoid becoming a meal for a predator.

So a jungle, even such a one as he awoke to find
himself in, held no terrors for a man who had been
raised by John Clayton, Lord Greystoke—who was
far better known as Tarzan of the Apes.

---

*Moran: A member of a Masai or Samburu war clan.
**Simi: East African sword with no guard to the hilt and a
pear-shaped blade.

Looking at his weapons, Bunduki hoped that his unknown rescuers had equipped his adoptive cousin at least as well. Given her Ben Pearson Marauder Take-Down hunting bow—custom built to a draw weight of seventy pounds—a supply of arrows and the Randall Model 1 Fighting knife which he had brought her as a Christmas present, Dawn could feed and, to a certain extent, protect herself until he could find her. The blood of Sir John and Lady Meriem Drummond-Clayton flowed through her veins and their jungle knowledge was bettered only by that of Lord and Lady Greystoke. Always a tomboy, Dawn had been on several of the family's expeditions before taking up her post at the University of Ambagasali and was capable of taking care of herself.

Eager as the blond giant might be to commence his search for Dawn, he was too wise to set about it in a hurried or impatient manner. The rash and incautious did not survive for long in a jungle. His every instinct warned him that the rule might apply even more strongly in his present situation. He was in a strange and unfamiliar type of country.

Just *how* strange, he could not yet say.

Seeing the red howler monkeys had suggested that he was no longer in Africa. Yet it was impossible for him to be anywhere else. He realized, however, that under the circumstances, he could not be sure of what was—or was not—possible.

He should not be dressed in the leopardskin loincloth. The big knife could have been hanging on his belt as he always carried it when on patrol, but the bow and arrows should have been locked in his study at the Wild Life Reserve's Headquarters.

So what was the answer?

Had Dawn and he been snatched from certain death and, in some equally miraculous manner, been transported without their knowledge to the jungles of South America?

If so, why had it been done and who could have had

the technical knowledge and equipment capable of doing it?

Even while thinking on those lines, Bunduki became conscious of the sensation of being watched. Instantly, he grew alert and started to search for the watcher.

There was a movement in an adjacent tree. Reaching for his bow, the blond giant turned his head to make a closer study. What he saw brought an even more puzzled frown to his face. He found himself looking at a predatory animal, but it was over thirty yards away and not a source of danger. The surprise came from a different reason. While the creature was feline, it was not—as might have been expected in a jungle that had red howler monkeys—a jaguar, mountain lion or ocelot. An ashy-grey in colour, its short-legged body was dappled with large, deeper grey areas which enclosed small dark spots and its tail looked long in proportion to its build.

As if becoming aware that it had been seen, the animal turned and darted away through the branches with as much ease and as swift as if it had been on the ground. That was, Bunduki realized, hardly surprising. *Neofelis nebulosa,* the clouded leopard, was arboreal by nature and only rarely descended to the ground. However, there were no clouded leopards in Africa, or South America. They were only found in the jungles of the East Indies and South-East Asia.

After continuing with what proved to be an abortive search for the watcher, whom he felt sure still had him under observation, Bunduki thrust the question, along with the puzzle of a jungle that held red howler monkeys *and* clouded leopards, from his mind. In the former case, he was willing to let the watcher take the initiative in making a closer acquaintance. The incessant inner suggestion that Dawn was somewhere to the north-west was too urgent for him to waste time on less vital considerations.

There was, Bunduki suddenly realized, one way in which he might learn of Dawn's exact whereabouts.

Although the *Mangani**—with whom Lord Greystoke
had lived until young manhood, following the death of
his parents while he was still a baby—had become extinct in the early 1950's, Tarzan and his family had
made use of their calls as a means of signalling to each
other. Some acoustic quality in the vocal range of the
Mangani allowed the sounds to carry for vast distances
through a jungle. So, even if Dawn was beyond the
range of a human voice, the challenge of a bull *Mangani*—being the farthest carrying of the calls, as it was
issued to give a warning of territorial rights—might
reach her. If she heard it, she would be able to identify
his voice and would know that he was looking for
her.

Filling his lungs, Bunduki flung back his head and
thundered out the awesome, roaring call. Twice more,
with an unabated volume, he sent the challenge echo-
ing through the jungle. Then he listened hopefully. A
small flock of greater curassows which were feeding at
the foot of the tree took off and flapped hurriedly
away. Nearby, a black rhinoceros lurched up from
where it had been sleeping and, with an explosive
snort, crashed away through the undergrowth. Not far
away, in another direction, what could only be a tiger
gave its throaty roar in answer to the challenge. At a
greater distance, elephants began to trumpet their defiance.

And then, from a long way off in the north-west,
rose a cry similar to that which Bunduki had given.

---

*Due to a lack of details when Mr. Commissioner Sanders,
C.M.G. (see the various volumes of biography by Edgar Wallace for information regarding Sanders of the River's career)
told Edgar Rice Burroughs about Tarzan and, later, in defer-
ence to Lord Greystoke's wishes—to prevent the *Mangani* from
interference and exploitation by human beings—they were described as being giant Anthropoid Apes. Since they are now extinct, Lord Greystoke has lifted his restrictions and it can be
stated that they were a species of *Australopithecus*. Neither
E.R.B. nor Mr Wallace disclosed the true identity of the infor-
mant, for reasons not unconnected with the British Government's Official Secrets Act.

For a moment, the blond giant wondered if his ears were playing tricks upon him. Then, as the distant call was repeated, he had the brief hope that it might be originating from a male member of his adoptive family. Certainly it had not been made by Dawn. She would have used the cry of a female *Mangani*. Nor was it likely to have come from Tarzan, Sir Paul, Korak the Killer,* or Armand. When Kenya had been granted its independence, they had known that there was no future for them if they had stayed there. So they had accepted David Innes' offer to join him and make a new life for themselves and their families in Pellucidar** Dawn and Bunduki had been included in the invitation. Being employed under contract by the Ambagasali Government, they had honored the agreements by staying on until suitable replacements could be hired.

So, with the rest of the Greystoke family already settled in their new homes at the Earth's core, the response to his challenge could not have been made by one of them. Yet Tarzan's exhaustive investigations during the mid-1960's had led him to believe that the *Mangani* were extinct.

That was, Bunduki concluded, just one more mystery to add to those which had already come to his attention since he awoke. It certainly did nothing to help him locate Dawn, unless she too had heard the distant call and was making her way towards it. So he decided that he would not allow the speculation to distract him any longer from his search.

Having reached his decision, the blond giant picked up his bow and climbed nimbly to the ground. On his arrival, still conscious of the feeling that his every move was being scrutinized, his right hand reached up and slid an arrow from the quiver on his back. Without

---

*Korak "The Killer," the Manganis' name for Sir John Drummond-Clayton.

**The story of David Innes is told in Edgar Rice Burroughs' "Pellucidar" books and Lord Greystoke's first visit there is described in: *TARZAN AT THE EARTH'S CORE.*

the need for him to look at what he was doing, he
rested its shaft on the arrow-shelf of the bow's handle
and and slipped the groove of the nock over the
string.

Once again, failing to locate the watcher, Bunduki
put the matter from his thoughts. However, he remained alert and his eyes were constantly on the move
as he started to walk in a north-westerly direction. As
he did so, he became aware of the pangs of a deep
hunger. It was as if he had nothing in his stomach
and intestines. Identifying a number of plants, bushes
and trees, although some were unfamiliar, he selected
such fruit and berries as he knew to be edible and ate
them while on the move. There was, however, a more
urgent need in the food line. From what he saw, filling
it should not be difficult for a man with his skill as a
hunter.

The variety of animals which Bunduki came across
proved to be an unending source of amazement and
conjecture. Once a troop of black and white Colobus
monkeys, like those in the Abedare Forest of Kenya,
hurled abuse at him from the trees. At the same time,
a small herd of white-spotted Axis deer fled as he had
seen their kind do during an expedition to India. Not a
mile away, while Hooloock gibbons swung from the
branches and fed in a fig tree, a large sounder of white-
lipped peccaries were foraging at its foot on the fruit
which were being dislodged. Later he heard the calls
of chimpanzees and of Asian jungle fowl. He saw
tracks left by bongo, giant forest hog and buffalo as
well as identifying—by sight—a South American three-
toed sloth and a Malayan tapir. Still further on, a bull
guided its harem and young away as a jaguar appeared
at the edge of the clearing in which they had been
grazing.

Birds, reptiles and smaller mammals were also
present in a similar geographically-confusing profusion. By their lack of fear, they were none of them
used to human beings. The only creatures that appeared to be absent, he noticed with relief, were

bothersome insects, ticks, leeches and other parasites.

It seemed to Bunduki that he had stumbled into a kind of vast zoological gardens, in which creatures from every continent had been gathered and were allowed to roam at will. Even *Mangani,* unless his imagination had been playing tricks upon him. That was possible, he had to admit. There had been no signs, nor sounds, of them apart from the very distant answer to his challenge.

Altogether the environment through which the blond giant was passing struck him as being something Dawn and he had frequently discussed and hoped to find as children. He could not even start to guess where on Earth it might be, which aroused another possibility— far-fetched as it might appear to be—for him to consider.

The time was almost noon and the continuing pangs of hunger caused Bunduki to set aside the train of thought which his summation had brought to mind. Instead, he started to hunt in deadly earnest. Gliding silently between the trees and through the undergrowth, with keen blue eyes constantly flickering glances from side to side, ears straining to catch the softest sound and nostrils testing the air—although his sense of smell was not so well developed as that of the other members of his adoptive family—he looked more like a predatory jungle creature than a civilized human being.

At last Bunduki found his prey. Halting in cover at the edge of a large clearing, he looked to where half a dozen greyish, somewhat squarely built creatures were feeding on the banks of a stream. They were capybara and, although rather large for his needs, made good eating. There was another point that appealed to him, as the former Chief Warden of a game reserve. Their species bred in such numbers that, particularly if his theory regarding his location was correct, the death of one would not seriously deplete the stock.

Standing erect and relaxed, with his left foot pointing towards the target, the blond giant extended his left arm and turned the bow from the nearly horizontal carrying position almost to vertical. The fingers of his bow-hand were curled around the pistol grip of the handle-riser, taking the pressure of the draw against the base of the thumb. His right elbow was raised outwards to shoulder level. Tucking the little finger of the draw-hand out of the way, he folded the remainder—with the nock of the arrow between the first and second digits—over the string. Utilizing his tremendously strong back and shoulder muscles, rather than those of his right arm, he drew the string and arrow rearwards.

Being a hunter, as opposed to a tournament-target archer, Bunduki favoured the high, or cheek draw. Tilting his head slightly to the right, until the second finger of his draw-hand was touching his cheeck just over the last tooth in his lower jaw, he attained his anchor point. He took aim swiftly and carefully, holding his breath to avoid the motion of his chest disturbing his posture. Then he relaxed the fingers of his right hand to accomplish a smooth release. Uncoiling from the arcs into which they had been drawn, the bow's upper and lower limbs caused the string to straighten and thrust the arrow forward.

Retaining his stance, the blond giant watched the thirty-one inch long arrow whistling through he air. It flew true and the capybara at which he had aimed, a young male, gave a convulsive bound as the one hundred and twenty-five grain, needle-sharp point spiked into its body. The razor-edged quadruple blades of the head cut onwards and collapsed the lungs in passing. Down went the stricken animal, its legs kicking. It was dead before its alarmed companions had plunged into the stream and swam away.

Resuming a more relaxed attitude, Bunduki strolled across the clearing. It was fringed by dense undergrowth that was pierced at several points by game trails. Reaching his prey, he lay the bow on the ground. Slipping off the quiver, as he meant to take a dip in the stream after he had eaten, he placed it alongside the bow. Then, as his right hand reached across to the Randall knife, he heard something which drove all thoughts of food from his head.

There was a rustling in the undergrowth to his left. A savage, snarling bellow rang out—followed by the scream of a terrified woman!

CHAPTER TWO

'Are You Also A Great Warrior?'

SEEING a shape appear at the top of the slope, the large black-maned lion rose from where it had been lazing in the shade of a clump of bushes. At its low, challenging growl, the rest of its pride interrupted their feeding on the carcass of the cow bison which they had killed.

At the sight of the lion, Dawn Drummond-Clayton came to a halt. It was, she told herself bitterly, her own fault that she should find herself in a such a precarious situation. After all she had seen that day, and with her practical experience, she ought to have been more careful. Instead of walking along engrossed in her thoughts, she should have stayed alert. If she had, the noises being made by the feeding pride would have warned her of their presence and she could have avoided them.

Of course, she went on, her preoccupation might be considered excusable under the circumstances.

Ever since Dawn had woken at sunrise, to find that she was lying on a ledge half way up the side of a rocky *kopje,** she had been forcing herself to accept very peculiar conditions. She had remembered M'Bili's murder and the Land Rover plunging into the Gambuti Gorge, but nothing more until waking to discover that she was alive and uninjured.

On first looking around, she had thought that she might be somewhere in the Ambagasali Wild Life Re-

*Kopje: Afrikaans word meaning a peak.

24

serve; although she could not imagine how she had come to be there. At every side the plains rolled away in gentle, undulating folds which were speckled with herds of herbivorous animals of many kinds and punctuated by *kopjes,* clumps of bushes and the occasional tree. The terrain was, in fact, reminiscent of what the male members of her family had jokingly referred to as the M.M.B.A.A.; the Miles and Miles of Bloody Awful Africa.

Having studied her surroundings, Dawn realized that she was not within the familiar bounds of the Reserve. The Reserve would have been hard put to equal the numbers of animals she had observed, and certainly could not have offered such a diversity of species. The very unusual variety of animals had caused her to have doubts as to whether she was even still in Africa. All of the normal plains' creatures had been in evidence; ostriches, secretary birds, kori bustards, warthogs, giraffes, buffalo and numerous types of antelope and gazelle from different parts of her home continent. Scattered among them had been nilgai and blackbuck from India. Giant anteaters, pronghorns, pampas and white-tail deer that were normally residents of North or South America had been mingling with them.

Various thoughts had been passing through her head as she stood identifying the different kinds of animals.

Could she be suffering from a dying illusion, or dreaming while unconscious from the injuries she had sustained in the crash?

Dawn doubted whether either supposition was the answer.

Then what had happened?

Where was she?

And, equally important, why had Bunduki not been brought with her?

Almost as a reply to the last question, the girl experienced a growing subconscious suggestion that her adoptive cousin was also alive and that she could find him somewhere in a jungle to the south-east.

Like the blond giant, Dawn had been puzzled by

the sensation. She had never felt anything so utterly demanding and compulsive. It was as if she had been subjected to post-hypnotic suggestion. While it was almost beyond her comprehension, she decided that it was no more so than any of the other inexplicable circumstances in which she found herself.

There was, Dawn had concluded, only one way to deal with the mystery. Accept the suggestion as valid and go to try and find Bunduki, who was almost certainly looking for her. Between them, they ought to be able to solve the other puzzles.

Having accepted that as her best course of action, Dawn had reviewed the situation in a calm and positive manner.

Whoever, or whatever, had saved her life must have had a sound and logical reason for doing so. Certainly they had given her adequate means of self-protection. In some way they had found and assembled her Ben Pearson Marauder Take-Down hunting bow. It had been at her side, with the eight-arrow bow-quiver attached and her shoulder-quiver. Altogether, they had supplied her with twenty-two fibre glass Micro-Flite arrows with four-blade Bear Razorhead points, all of which were most acceptable in her present situation. Nor would her Randall Model 1 fighting knife come amiss. It was hanging sheathed on the belt of the garments which had replaced the blouse, jeans and moccasins she had been wearing in the Land Rover.

In addition to arming her, the mysterious rescuers had given her a way of satisfying the sensation of complete emptiness in her stomach. There had been a small packet, wrapped in the skin of a Thomson's gazelle, with her bow. Opening it, she had found that it contained some *biltong** and *pemmican.*** There had even

---

*Biltong: Afrikaans' name for sun-dried meat. The Americans call it "jerky."

**Pemmican: A North American Indian food made from buffalo meat, or venison, which is dried, mixed with tallow—the harder, coarser of the body's fats—and berries, all pounded and

been a small stream near the foot of the *kopje* so that she had been able to quench her thirst.

Leaving the vicinity of the *kopje,* after having eaten a good meal, Dawn had started to walk in a south-easterly direction. She had had the sensation of being watched by something other than the animals, but had not been able to locate the person, or persons, responsible. Although the scrutiny had continued, nothing had come of it. So she had decided to let the observers make the first move in the matter of estab-lishing contact. They had not offered to do so, but she soon had other things to require her attention. In addi-tion to the herbivorous animals, there were other and more dangerous creatures to be taken into consider-ation. There had been other lions, a couple of cheetahs, a family of Cape hunting dogs and, far away, what she had taken to be a pack of wolves, but she had avoided coming too close to any of them.

With the exception of the modern materials used in the construction of her weapons, Dawn seemed to blend perfectly into the primitive nature of her surroundings. Five foot eight inches in height, with the kind of a figure that many a sex-symbol movie star needed arti-ficial aids to attain—bust, 38; waist, 20; hips, 36—she presented a picture of primitive, savage womanhood. Kept short for convenience, her curly tawny hair formed a frame to set off classically beautiful features. Tanned to a rich golden bronze, like all the exposed portions of her gorgeous body and legs, her face de-noted breeding, intelligence, strength of will and de-termination. Power-packed, yet not unfeminine mus-cles, rippled under her sleek skin and she moved with the fluid grace of a trained athlete.

While most flattering to her appearance, the cloth-ing which had replaced her garments was anything but civilized. She was now wearing a very short, simple dress made from the soft hide of a cow eland. It was

---

pressed tightly together to form a cake. Like biltong, or jerky, it is nutritious and will keep in good condition for a long time without refrigeration.

one-piece, sleeveless from the waist to its extremely daring décolleté, laced with leather thongs and clung to the splendid contours of her torso and hips as if moulded upon them. The dress, a pair of leopard-skin briefs, an archer's armguard, a pigskin bowman's glove and the belt were her sole ensemble.

Despite the scanty nature of her attire, armed as she was, Dawn felt sure that she could survive until she had found her adoptive cousin. If she could not, she would be unworthy of her heritage. Not only had her mother and father been espionage agents in German-occupied Europe throughout much of World War II, facing great dangers and living in the shadow of a very painful death if they had been captured, but her grandparents had survived for many years during their youth in the jungles of Africa. With a bloodline like that, she ought to be self-sufficient even in such puzzling and disturbing circumstances. What was more, she had had excellent training for whatever might lie ahead.

Always something of a tomboy, Dawn had insisted upon duplicating the lessons in self defense and weapon handling received by her—at that time—almost inseparable companion, Bunduki. On being sent to Roedean for her education, she had thrown herself whole-heartedly into every permissible kind of sport and had excelled at them all. However, like her adoptive cousin, she had grown disenchanted by the blatantly one-sided political bias of the international sporting bodies. So, although of world class as an athlete, gymnast and swimmer, she too had refused to enter competitions. For all that, she had kept up her training and was in the peak of physical condition.

There were, however, limits to how far her physical prowess could protect her. It would not, for instance, save her if the big, black-maned lion should attack.

Despite the perilous nature of her predicament, Dawn did not panic. Instead, she turned her attention to thinking of how she might extract herself from it. To turn and run would almost certainly arouse the instinct

which every predatory creature had to chase anything
that fled from it. During a charge, a lion could attain a
speed of around fifty miles per hour. So, especially
while she was encumbered by the bow and arrows—
which she had no desire to discard—even though a distance of slightly over thirty yards was separating them,
she could not hope to outrun the lion. Nor was there
a tree close enough for her to be able to seek refuge
in its branches.

Standing perfectly still, Dawn made no attempt to
raise her bow into the shooting position. While she
had not been so incautious that she had been carrying
it without an arrow nocked to the string, she realized
that it would be inadequate in the event of the lion
making a charge.

No arrow, even when loosed from a bow which
drew seventy pounds and carrying a modern four-
bladed hunting point, had the *stopping* power of a
medium to heavy calibre rifle. If a lion was hit by a
heavy enough bullet, it would be knocked from its feet
and so allow the delivery of a second round. An arrow could not do that, as the force of the powder
charge behind the bullet was far greater than the propulsive effect of any practical bow.

Of course, the *killing* power of an arrow's four-
bladed point was even more effective than that of a bullet under certain conditions. Cutting a path almost two
inches wide as it entered the animal's body, the arrow
was almost certain to cause death by bleeding—but,
unless it was placed with great accuracy and into a vital
area, not quickly enough to end a charge.

A hit in the head, providing it caught the brain, or
through the chest cavity to tear apart the heart or the
lungs, would cause almost instant death. However, she
felt disinclined to chance aiming for such small targets
when they would be approaching her at speed. Even a
slight error in alignment would be fatal to her. While
the wounded beast might—in fact, probably would—
die, it would not do so before having reached and
either seriously injured or killed her.

Studying the great cat, Dawn began to draw conclusions based upon her past experiences and what she had been taught about the habits of *Panthera Leo*. As one of her instructors had been her adoptive great-grandfather—who had raised and trained *Jad-Bal-Ja,* the Golden Lion and had had plenty to do with them in the wild—she felt sure that she could rely upon the information.

Taking into consideration the big male's obviously well filled stomach and the fact that the rest of the pride were being allowed to feed from the kill—which, even in the stress of the moment, she had noticed appeared to be a North American bison—she decided that it must already have eaten its fill. In which case, unless it differed greatly from those others of its kind with which she had come into contact, it was no longer hungry, and would be disinclined to exert itself without considerable provocation.

"All right, *numa*," Dawn breathed, using the *Manganis'* word for a lion. "I won't provoke you. I'm going away and, unless you want this arrow down your throat, you won't try to stop me."

Having delivered the *sotto voce* comment, although she knew that the beast would not have understood even if it had heard, the girl made a slow and tentative step to the rear. At her first movement, the lion tensed and its tail began to swing from side to side.

Dawn came to an immediate halt, ready to raise and draw the bow!

Standing like a statue, the girl kept her hazel eyes on the lion's, fixing them in a stare as unblinking as its own. Almost thirty seconds dragged by on leaden feet, seeming to be *much* longer, before the great cat's tail ceased its swinging and it looked away from her unremitting scrutiny.

Dawn took another step!

Although the lion's eyes returned to her, there was no other response from it. So, without turning her back on it, she continued to retreat. She went unhurriedly, wanting to make sure that she did not trip and fall as much as to avoid any sudden motions that would alarm it. The lion watched her go and, as she had hoped, made no attempt to follow. Instead, even before she had passed out of sight over the top of the slope, it slumped back into the shade of the bushes. Seeing that the head of their pride was settling down, the three lionesses and their cubs resumed the interrupted meal.

Once beyond the lion's range of vision, Dawn stopped and sucked in a long, deep breath. Although she had extracted herself from the predicament without difficulty, she did not minimize how dangerous it had been. If the lion had been hungry, she would not have escaped so easily. Taking her right hand from the bow's string and supporting the arrow with her left, she wiped away the film of perspiration that had formed on her brow. While she was doing it, the memory of something that she had been told as a child came to mind.

"If Esmeralda* was right and servants sweat, gentlemen perspire, but ladies only glow," Dawn thought with a smile, "I can't be a lady. This is either sweat, or the wettest 'glow' I've ever seen."

Having delivered that sentiment, which served to relieve the tension left by what she knew had been a narrow escape, Dawn returned her hand to the nock of the arrow and resumed her journey. However, she had taken the warning to heart, and let neither her curiosity over the strange circumstances of her rescue from the Land Rover, nor the continuing sensation of being kept under observation, interfere with her vigilance.

After about an hour had passed without incident, other than seeing game in the same bewildering profusion, a column of smoke attracted Dawn's attention. It was some distance away, to the east, but had the appearance of rising from a camp fire.

The sight presented Dawn with a problem. To go to the source of the smoke would take her away from

*Esmeralda Moreland, Lady Greystoke's nurse and maid.

the direction in which her instincts suggested she would find Bunduki. However, unless a certain theory which she had been considering just before the meeting with the lion should prove to be correct, whoever had made the fire might help her in the search. Even if her supposition was right, provided she exercised caution, she could gain some useful information. With that in mind, she turned to the east and made for the smoke.

Long before Dawn was within sight of her destination, her way was barred by a wide chasm through which raced the waters of a river. To the south-east, about a mile away, the plains began to merge with scrub and woodland that she sensed was the outer limits of the jungle in which—if her subconscious feelings were true—she would locate Bunduki. So she paused, undecided as to whether she should go there or try to find a way across the river and make for the fire.

While the girl was considering what to do, she became aware that three mounted figures had come into view at the top of a slope on the other side of the chasm. Watching them riding towards the edge and thinking of the theory which she had been formulating with regards to her whereabouts, she was not sorry that a gap of about fifty yards would be separating her from them. While everything about them seemed to be further evidence that she was no longer in any part of Africa as she knew it, nothing supplied a clue as to where she might be.

The trio, a woman and two men, were mounted on horse-like animals. The ears, mane and patterning of black and white stripes on the smaller man's beast were suggestive of a Grant's zebra. Brown in colour, taller and of better quality, the other two animals had black and cream striping on the head, neck and shoulders only. The long extinct quaggas of South Africa had been coloured and marked in such a fashion. In fact, they all bore the same kind of resemblance to wild zebras as a thoroughbred Arabian stallion bore to a tarpon or a Przewalski's horse, the progenitors of the

domestic breeds. Apparently the three riders' mounts
had evolved from varieties of zebra which had been
bred for long enough in captivity to have developed into riding strains far superior to the original wild stock.

Not that Dawn devoted too much of her attention
to the animals. She was finding the appearances of
their riders to be of even greater interest.

Sitting her mount with the easy grace of an excellent
rider, the woman was bronzed, black-haired and very
beautiful. Yet, for all the sensual pout to her full lips,
her dark eyes and expression suggested a cruel and
imperious nature. She was about an inch taller than
Dawn and would probably exceed the girl's age, twen-
ty-one, by six or seven years. Her shoulder long tresses
were held back by a broad band of what looked like
gold lamé fabric. The halter which was flimsily covering the full, firm thirty-nine inches of her bosom and
the brief skirt which emphasised the contours of her
thirty-seven inch hips and buttocks were made from a
mesh of the same material. Her legs were in keeping
with the rest of her magnificent figure. Criss-crossing
her calves to just below the knees, the straps of her
sandals were gold in colour. About her bare, twenty
inch, waist was a belt comprised of gold and silver
discs. It supported the scabbard of an ivory hilted
sword shaped like a Roman soldier's *gladius*. Apart
from a wide gold bracelet on her right wrist, she had
no jewellery. Her right hand was holding the reins and
the left rested on the hilt of the sword as she arrogantly returned the girl's scrutiny.

The man on the woman's left was tall, middle-aged
and well built. Covering his skull, so that only his
hard, cruel face was exposed, his metal helmet was
embossed on each side with a zebra's head. It was
topped by a crest that might have come from the mane
of his mount. His swarthy features had harsh lines,
and a long, drooping moustache did little to soften the
cruel set of his thin lips. He had on a breast-plate of
polished leather carved ornately with some kind of
design, over what appeared to be a white silk shirt. The

kilt he was wearing looked as though it was made of leather. Greaves of that material, etched decoratively, protected his shins and he had sandals on his feet. The sword sheathed on the left side of his belt, which was formed from all gold discs, was of the same design as the woman's, but heavier and longer. Grasped at its point of balance, the butt of a nine foot long lance was resting in the cup attached for that purpose to his right side stirrup.

Although dressed in much the same way as the tall man, the second male rider was middle-sized, stocky and obviously of a lower social status. No crest adorned his helmet, nor was there any engraving on his breast-plate and greaves. The sword he was carrying had a plain wooden hilt and was his only weapon.

Not only the man's dress and mount suggested that he was of a subordinate rank, his behaviour proved it. Althugh his companions had halted and were staring across the chasm, he directed only the briefest glance at Dawn. Then he reined his zebra—she had decided to give the animals such a title—around in a half circle and stopped it within reaching distance of the woman's right hand.

The girl had no need to ponder over the second man's actions. A wooden framework was attached to the cantle of his saddle, which—like those of his companions, although theirs were of a better quality—resembled a low horned, double girthed Texas range rig, extending to rest on the zebra's rump. On the crossbar, with its head covered by a finely decorated leather hood that was designed to display its prominent crest of feathers, perched an enormous bird of prey. Its great size, body's shape, mottled grey upper surfaces, black chest, white underparts, shortish, powerful, very deep but comparatively narrow curved beak, thick legs and massive claws told her that it was a harpy eagle of some kind.

Ignoring the third member of their party and the bird, the woman and the taller man were subjecting Dawn to mutually long examinations. Then they exchanged glances, each nodding as if they had reached some unspoken agreement. Having done so, the man returned his gaze to the girl, raking her from head to foot. There was lust and worse in his scrutiny. Then he stiffened slightly and swung his eyes to look north on her side of the chasm.

Before Dawn could turn her head in that direction, more riders came into sight on the rim. Two women and four men, clad, armed and mounted in a similar manner to her examiners, but in a slightly less opulent fashion. The women, both beautiful and shapely, had on garments of silver lamé. While the taller of the women, and all the men, wore greaves, the second woman copied, in silver, the gold-clad beauty's taste in footwear. The animals they were sitting looked like the larger Grevy's species of zebra; having numerous narrow black stripes, but no gridiron pattern of transverse bars on the hind quarters that identified the Grant's variety.

Studying the newcomers, Dawn was relieved to see that none of them carried bows and arrows. They all appeared to be interested in her, but did not offer to ride any closer. Instead, they began to talk quietly amongst themselves. Then the woman without the greaves rose on her stirrups. Shielding her eyes with her right hand, she stared in a more noticeable fashion than the tall man had done across the chasm and to the north.

"Who are you?" called the man, bringing his attention back to the girl.

The words served to jolt Dawn's thoughts away from the manner in which the shorter of the women on the rim was acting.

They had been spoken in English!

Or had they?

Dawn sensed that her brain had been translating the man's question automatically, as it did when she was using one of the foreign languages with which she was acquainted.

"My name is 'Dawn,'" the girl found herself ansering and guessed that, no matter what language she was using, the people across the chasm could understand her.

That was, Dawn decided, pretty conclusive proof of her theory's validity.

"Are you alone?" demanded the black-haired woman, in a husky contralto voice that contrived to be domineering as well as sultry, scanning the terrain around Dawn.

"My cousin—and many of our warriors—are close by," the girl bluffed, wishing she had avoided the slight hesitation while increasing the size of hers and Bunduki's party. "If I call for them, they will come quickly."

"To which nation do you belong?" the man inquired, continuing to dart glances at the north as if expecting to see something in that direction. "You don't dress like an Amazon and you're not a Gruziak, or a Telonga."

Although Dawn knew that the original Amazons had been a nation of female warriors in Ancient Greece, she had never heard of peoples called the Gruziak or the Telonga.

"I belong to the people of Tarzan of the Apes," the girl replied, hoping to obtain some clue as to where she was.

In the course of an exceptionally eventful life, Lord Greystoke had travelled extensively and had been in contact with several strange, previously undiscovered races. Perhaps he had come across the people to whom her interrogators belonged, although she could not recollect him ever having mentioned them.

"And who, or *what* might this Tarzan of the—Apes —be?" the woman asked haughtily, fumbling with the word "Apes" as if it was not familiar.

Once again, Dawn decided not to tell the exact truth. It would take too long to tell the full story and describe her exact relationship with Lord and Lady Greystoke. In fact, the latter might be beyond her audience's comprehension. With their parents dead,

Captain Hugh "Bulldog" Drummond* had not been able to raise or care for his younger brother, John, in an adequate manner. So his second cousin, Lord Greystoke,** had adopted the youngster as his son and given him the name Drummond-Clayton.†

However, Dawn doubted whether the couple would appreciate such a relationship as an adoptive great-granddaughter. That would be particularly so if the woman was only pretending to be ignorant of Tarzan's identity and had actually met him. Few people knew about the Kavurus' longevity pills that had come into his possession and had been shared amongst his family. These tablets had halted the aging processes of the human body and had granted the recipients—barring accidental death, suicide or murder—what amounted to immortality. To avoid arousing unwanted interest, due to the fact that they all appeared to be in their late twenties and showed no signs of getting older, the family had resorted to make-up when receiving visits by any but very close and trusted friends or when travelling. Dawn had often thought, not without amusement, that her mother, grandmother and Lady Greystoke must be almost the only women in the world who deliberately sought to make themselves look older.

"He is my father and the chief of all our people," Dawn answered, having decided that such a relationship—the latter part of which was true—might be more

*Captain Hugh "Bulldog" Drummond's biography is recorded in the books of H.C. "Sapper" Melville and Gerald Fairlie, although they were requested not to make any mention of his younger brother to avoid reprisals against John by Carl Petersen.

**The family ties between Lord Greystoke and the Drummond brothers are explained in detail by fictionist genealogist Philip José Farmer in: *TARZAN ALIVE*.

†At Lord Greystoke's request and in the interests of producing a fast-moving story without extensive explanations, Mr. Burroughs did not reveal John Drummond-Clayton's exact status when writing *THE SON OF TARZAN*. However, permission now having been granted, this has been clarified in the above mentioned work by Mr. Farmer.

acceptable and suitably impressive. "He and all my people are great warriors and mighty archers."

As the girl said the final words, she gestured with the bow to emphasise their meaning. None of the riders were armed in such a fashion and she did not know if they would understand the term. However, having had his attention drawn to it, the tall man was staring at the powerful weapon and displaying great interest. Clearly he knew what it was, but now realized that it differed from any other bow that he had seen. That, Dawn told herself, was not surprising.

"Are *you* also a great warrior?" the woman challenged.

"If I need to be," Dawn answered, her feminine feelings bristling with annoyance at the other's attitude.

Raising his eyes from the bow, the tall man subjected Dawn to another scrutiny. She noticed the difference in his behaviour. It seemed that he was no longer primarily interested in her physical attractions, but was sizing her up in the light of her statement.

"Why don't you call for your cousin and his warriors to join you?" he finally suggested, twisting his features into what he probably imagined was a friendly smile. "If you came upstream, there is a place where we can cross and make friends."

On hearing the girl's response to her question, the woman had snapped her gaze to the tall man and was studying him in a calculating, almost suspicious seeming, fashion. Then she stared back at Dawn, but in a less mocking and more hostile manner.

"Yes, why don't you?" the gold-clad beauty went on, but there was neither friendship nor a welcome in her voice. "We have had a successful hunt and there is more than enough meat for you, your cousin—and all his *many* warriors."

There was something in the contralto tones that warned Dawn that her bluff had failed and the speaker realized she was alone. No matter how genuine the man's invitation might have been, the woman did not duplicate it. For some reason, she had turned from being mocking and derisive into a bitter enemy. Apparently she had detected some motive of which she did not approve in the man's change of attitude towards the girl.

In addition to carrying on the conversation, Dawn had been keeping the second party of riders under observation. They were, in her opinion, still paying too much attention to the north of her position. It was as if, like the tall man, they were expecting to see something in that direction.

Or *somebody!*

Suddenly, the smaller of the women in the silver garments pointed in an excited manner. Looking in the direction she was indicating, Dawn realized that the couple had been holding her attention deliberately. They had hoped to prevent her noticing a pair of riders who had topped a ridge about half a mile away. Mounted on zebras, the two men were dressed in the same way as the eagle's attendant and were armed with lances. Even as the girl located them, they urged their mounts forward at a faster pace.

All too well Dawn realized what the riders' presence on her side of the river meant. Her every instinct gave warning that it would be unwise to fall into their hands. Up to that moment, she had believed that she had nothing to fear from the zebra-riding people. None of them were carrying bows and the distance was too great for a lance, even if it had been designed for throwing, to be of any serious danger. She could have watched its flight and dodged it.

The approaching pair had changed the situation drastically. They were on Dawn's side of the chasm and would travel much faster than she could on foot. For all that, she intended to try and reach the woodland. If their mounts were anything to go by, the people were plainsdwellers and, once among the trees, she would have an advantage over them.

With that in mind, Dawn swung on her heel and started to run. She was still carrying the bow with an arrow nocked to the string. To have removed and returned it to the quiver on her back would have taken seconds which might prove vital to her escape. So she accepted the awkwardness of running with it in a position of readiness.

Letting out a furious exclamation, the tall man signalled for the riders to move faster. With her beautiful features twisted into lines of savage satisfaction, the woman by his side let the one-piece reins fall on to her mount's neck. Reaching out with her right hand, she plucked the hood from the head of the harpy eagle.

"Gaze-ho!" she snapped.

Hearing the familiar command, following the removal of the hood which had acted as a blindfold, the enormous bird crouched on its perch. Its powerful body was quivering with eagerness and its head swung until the cruel red eyes were attracted by Dawn's fleeing figure.

"What are you do——?" the tall man began, twisting on his saddle to glare at his female companion. Seeing what she was doing, he continued hastily, "No! I want her ali——!"

"Kill!" ordered the woman, ignoring the protest.

Concentrating on the ground over which she was speeding, so as to avoid stepping into a hole or on a stone that might turn under her foot and cause her to stumble, Dawn suddenly became aware of the danger that was approaching. It was coming from a source much closer than the two riders who were galloping in her direction. She heard the swishing of heavy wings and knew instantly what the sound portended.

It was, the girl told herself, something that she ought to have expected and taken into account. Everything about the eagle had pointed to it having been trained for falconry. Instead of thinking about the ease with which she could have avoided a thrown lance, or growing complacent because the riders did not carry bows, she should have guessed how they could attempt to ensure her capture. While she might be safe from the lances, the eagle could fly across the chasm and reach her without any difficulty.

Throwing a quick glance at the two riders, Dawn wondered if she could turn, deal with the bird, and still beat them to the woodland. Not that, she realized, she had any real choice in the matter. She might—and it would only just be *might*—outrun the men, but the bird would be upon her long before she attained the safety of the trees.

However, if Dawn halted for long enough to drive away or kill the eagle, the two men would arrive and cut her off.

CHAPTER THREE

You Take Woman. Go!

ALMOST before the echoes of the scream had ceased, Bunduki was bending to retrieve his bow. This time, however, he liberated an arrow from the bow-quiver and made his weapon ready for use. All the time his hands were moving, he watched the left side of the clearing.

As yet, the dense nature of the bushes was preventing the blond giant from seeing the person who had screamed. Nor could he discover the cause of her alarm. With the wind, what there was of it, blowing from the north, his sense of smell was of no assistance in gathering further information. However, his ears suggested that there was more than one pursuer.

Suddenly, a feminine figure dashed from the mouth of the game trail. Although Bunduki had not expected her to be Dawn, it was still something of a relief when a stranger came into view.

Long, straight black hair streamed behind the running girl and her very pretty face was distorted by an expression of horror. She was brown skinned, like a Polynesian, about five-foot-three in height and possessed exceptionally well-developed contours. They were made all the more obvious due to the skimpy manner in which she was dressed. Her clothing consisted of a short skirt made from twisted strands of grass—and not too many of them—and a small halter that looked like a strip of colobus monkey's skin. Unarmed, and clearly very frightened, she sped recklessly across the open ground. Instead of giving any indica-

42

tion that she was aware of the blond giant's presence, she ran towards the river.

"This way!" Bunduki called, hoping that she would understand.

At the sound of his voice, the girl showed her first sign of realizing that another human being was close by. Staring at Bunduki, she gave a croaking cry of mingled alarm and relief. She started to swerve in his direction, tripped and went sprawling to the ground. After rolling over a couple of times, she halted in a crouching posture and covered her face with her arms. Sobs of terror and exhaustion shook at her scantily covered and voluptuous little body.

Striding forward, Bunduki had just reached the girl when the first of her pursuers emerged from the undergrowth. Studying the creature, he could understand the reason for her panic-stricken flight.

Bunduki's first thought was that the creature might be a gorilla, but a second look led him to revise his opinion. While it was coated with coarse brown hair and had the short-necked, projecting face of an ape, it ran with an upright stance and with an ease that no gorilla or chimpanzee could duplicate.

Other details began to leap to Bunduki's attention. The creature's broad shoulders and heavily muscled arms suggested that it travelled by brachiation, swinging from branch to branch through the trees. Yet its legs were long and straight, with feet more suited to bipedal walking or running on the ground. In height, it just topped six foot. While anything but puny, weighing maybe three hundred pounds, it lacked the massive bulk of a bull gorilla. Still more significantly, as far as identification was concerned, it was carrying a six foot long, fairly straight branch which had been broken to leave a sharp point at the forward end. From the way the creature was handling the branch, he—there was no doubt as to the sex—was aware of its potential as a rudimentary, yet effective spear.

No gorilla knew how to make, nor use, weapons. Even the more intelligent chimpanzee would only

throw or wield a stick, wildly, and none too effectively
for defense.

The fact that the creature was armed in such a way
might prove it was not a gorilla, but it also produced
an argument to the alternative which had come to
Bunduki's mind. If he had not seen the branch-spear,
he would have thought that it was an *Australopithecus*. One of the same species which his adoptive father's
American biographer had always referred to as the
Great Anthropoid Apes, but who had really been an
omnivorous pre-human phase of *hominid* evolution.
Somewhat smaller and lighter than the gorilla, which
had frequently shared their domains,* the *Mangani*
had possessed a higher standard of intelligence. However, although Lord Greystoke had once taught some
of them to row a boat, those of the race with whom
he had been associated did not know how to make, or
even use, such a simple weapon as the branch-spear.

Thrusting aside his thoughts on the creature's possible identity, the blond giant prepared to deal with him.
Whether he was a more advanced kind of *Australopithecus,* or some later species like *Homo Erectus Erectus***
—which, it has been established, was capable of
making and using primitive tools—he was certainly
dangerous.

At the sight of Bunduki moving protectively between
him and the girl, the man-ape—which was the most
apt description the blond giant could think of—came
to a halt.

Three more of the creatures, all just as obviously
masculine, lumbered from the game trail. Two were
smaller than the first, reddish brown in colour and
armed with branch-spears. Larger and heavier than the

---

*Due to the similarity to their appearances and because the
true status of the *Mangani* had yet to be discovered, it is possible that they were responsible for most of the reports of gorillas attacking natives and abducting their women.

**Bunduki later established that they were a transitory stage
between *Australopithecus* and *Homo Erectus Erectus* and not
the type of Mangani known to Tarzan.

rest, the fourth was almost black and grasped a thick, knobbly three-foot length of tree root in the manner of a club. Clearly he was the leader of the group. Although he had been bringing up the rear, he pushed to the front. From his lips, as they advanced, came three rumbling, almost grunting sounds.

Much to Bunduki's surprise, he found that he could understand the big male's guttural words.

"*Bul-Mok* kill!" the man-ape had announced, his name meaning, "Big Father."

"Keep away, or *Tar-Ara* kill!"

To add to Bunduki's astonishment, he found that he was able to answer the threat in the same kind of primitive tongue. Although he had been encouraged by his adoptive parents to make the most of his facility for learning languages, he had not had the opportunity to acquire any extensive knowledge of *Mangani*. Nor, with them being so close to extinction, had there seemed to be any point in him doing so.

Not that the blond giant believed he was consciously speaking the *Mangani* dialect when he gave the warning and translated his name as "White Lightning." For some reason that he could not comprehend, his brain was registering the thoughts in English and they were leaving his mouth in the form of simple, yet alien word-sounds.

Clearly the men-apes were puzzled at meeting a human being who was able to address them in their own primitive tongue. They came to a stop, with the younger males lowering their weapons. They were waiting to see how their father wanted the situation handled.

Deep growls rumbled in *Bul-Mok's* throat and he swayed uncertainly on his spread apart feet. Glaring at the blond giant, he tried to decide what would be his best line of action. Faced with a dangerous creature of another species, the usual thing would have been for him and his sons to launch a mass attack. However, against one of their own kind who had strayed into their territory, *Bul-Mok*—in his capacity as dominant male of the family—alone must assert his authority.

Although Bunduki did not know it, *Bul-Mok* had never seen a human being until coming across the girl. While puzzled by the blond giant's hairless body and strange features, the big man-ape was unable to decide whether he could be classed as a *Mangani* or not. The answer to the puzzle would tell *Bul-Mok* how to deal with the intruder.

"This *Bul-Mok's* land!" the dominant male stated, beating at hus chest with his left fist. *"Bul-Mok* kill!"

"Tar-Ara mighty fighter," Bunduki countered, although holding the bow prevented him from repeating the other's gesture. "Not afraid of *Bul-Mok!"*

Throwing back his head, the dominant male thundered out a challenge. There was no doubt about it, Bunduki told himself. It was the call of a bull *Mangani*. What was more, he knew how he must respond. While he had learned only a little of the *Manganis'* simple language, he could make all of the various signal calls. So he replied in kind and his deep-throated roar shattered the air.

Hearing the awesome sound so close above her, the girl crouching at Bunduki's feet looked up. A low moan burst from her as she realized that the second bellow, no less savage in timbre than the one which had preceded it, must have been made by the giant white man. Burying her face in her hands once more, she moaned incoherently and tried to make herself even smaller.

Discovering that the strange white creature not only spoke *Mangani* but made the correct response to the challenge roar was disconcerting to *Bul-Mok*. It presented a situation which severely taxed his limited intelligence and reasoning powers.

Should he order his sons to charge?

Or must he treat the intruder as a trespasser of their own kind, strange-looking but a *Mangani* for all that, who must be dealt with by himself?

All *Bul-Mok's* instincts warned him that the big

stranger was a powerful and dangerous challenger. Bearing that in mind, the man-ape sought for a way to avoid a direct confrontation—but without letting it be apparent to the other members of his family that he was doing so. His eyes roamed the clearing, avoiding having to meet *Tar-Ara's* gaze, coming to rest on the dead capybara. Returning his attention to the blond giant, he decided to offer a compromise which, if accepted, would leave the next move to his oldest son.

It was a shrewd piece of reasoning for a *Mangani*. *Bal-Tak,* 'First Born,' was rapidly approaching the point when he would make a bid to overthrow *Bul-Mok* and assume control of the family group. Seeing how he fared against *Tar-Ara* would allow the dominant male to estimate his potential as a rival.

"We take food," *Bul-Mok* offered. "You take woman. *Go!*"

"Woman mine. Food mine!" Bunduki snapped back. "*You* go!"

Greed and selfishness had not prompted the hostile answer. While Bunduki still was not absolutely sure of the kind of sub-human *hominids* he was up against, he could imagine how they would react to any suggestion of weakness on his part. That was how the younger males would have regarded his acceptance of their father's offer. Like most primates, the *Mangani* lived in social groups controlled by a male hierarchy. The largest, strongest male was the leader with the next toughest ranking second and so on down the scale. Each member could only retain, or improve, his position in the community by bluff or actual fighting prowess.

For Bunduki to have yielded would have been construed as an admission of inferiority to *Bul-Mok*. Even if he had allowed the big blond and the girl to go, the next largest of the males would have been compelled to make a challenge and establish his standing in the group. By acting as he had, Bunduki was hoping that he would have only the leader to contend with.

Confronted with such open and direct defiance, *Bul-Mok* was placed in a difficult position. His superiority was being threatened in the fashion of the *Mangani*. That ruled out the possibility of him ordering his sons to attack *Tar-Ara*. So he must act on his own, or he would be in danger of losing his dominance over the family group. With that not unimportant consideration in mind, he took a firmer grip on his club.

"*Bul-Mok* kill!" the *Mangani* thundered, swinging the heavy weapon over his head and lumbering forward.

Instantly, Bunduki brought the bow to the shooting position and made his draw with smoothly flowing speed. With the arrow at its anchor point, he sighted on the centre of *Bul-Mok's* broad chest.

Still too far away for his club to be of any use, the dominant *Mangani's* life hung on a very delicate balance. If any of his sons had made a move to help him, he would have died. As it was, having no desire to kill him if it could be avoided, the blond giant did not release the arrow. The three younger bulls seemed content to leave matters in their father's hands. *Bul-Mok's* lack of concern over the threat of the arrow suggested that such a weapon was unknown to him. If he was killed in what his sons might regard as an inexplicable manner, they could be frightened into making a mass attack. Even utilizing the benefits of the bow-quiver for rapidity of reloading, or wielding his bowie knife—which would probably be an equally unknown factor to the *Mangani*—he doubted whether he would be able to fight off all three of them. Certainly, while doing it, and in the event of being successful, he would receive wounds which could incapacitate him and prevent him from continuing his search for Dawn until he had recovered.

Bunduki decided that he could avert the possibility by impressing them with his physical prowess. It would have a far greater effect than would be achieved by killing with a means that they might not be able to comprehend. To defeat the dominant male with his bare hands was the best way to attain his ends.

Changing his point of aim, Bunduki loosed the arrow. It flashed forward to strike the bulbous upper end of the club. Impaling it, the buff-coloured fiber glass shaft wrenched the weapon from *Bul-Mok's* hands. A startled, almost barking exclamation burst from the dominant male's lips and he sprang backwards in alarm. Staring at the arrow, which was projecting through the head of the club, the other three bulls retreated just as hurriedly.

Having regained her breath and discovered that she was still alive and unharmed, the girl had remained in the crouching position, but she was now watching her defender with awe and considerable interest. Although her people told stories about them, few could claim to have seen the "Hairy Men" and then only from a distance and with the width of the Big River between them. Certainly not even the most boastful could claim to be able to speak the "Hairy Men's" language, yet the blond stranger apparently could do so.

Knowing the purpose of the bow, although she had never seen one as powerful as that held by her giant rescuer, the girl had expected him to send its arrow into the "Hairy Man's" chest. She was puzzled when he deliberately contented himself with knocking the club from the advancing bull's hands. What he did next changed her perturbation into active alarm.

Without taking his eyes from the *Mangani,* Bunduki laid his bow on the ground alongside the girl and walked by her. To her horror, he made no attempt to draw the big knife that was hanging from his belt.

"Go!" the blond giant ordered, pointing to the left side of the clearing.

Bul-Mok had been afraid of the intruder's strange weapon, realizing that it had qualities beyond anything his club or a branch-spear possessed. Seeing that *Tar-Ara* had laid it down, the dominant male decided that he could take the chance of making another attack.

At six-foot-five, size and weight were in his favour. So were the big canine teeth in his powerful jaws. Once he came to close quarters, he would be avenged. With a menacing roar, he bounded forward and his huge hands reached out ready to take hold.

Watching *Bul-Mok* bearing down on him, Bunduki felt confident of victory. The *Mangani* might have learned how to make and use primitive weapons, but they obviously still relied upon brute strength when fighting bare-handed. With his very thorough education in various forms of self defense and unarmed combat, the blond giant knew a number of excellent ways to handle such bull-headed tactics.

Taking a couple of long strides, to make sure he was well clear of the girl, Bunduki flashed up his hands to grasp *Bul-Mok's* right wrist. Turning the trapped hand palm upwards, he pivoted swiftly until his back was to the *Mangani* and the elbow of the fur-covered arm rested on his left shoulder. By sinking to his right knee and levering on the arm, he catapulated *Bul-Mok* over him. Turning a half somersault, with the blond giant still holding his wrist, the *Mangani* alighted on his back with a bone-jarring thud. Nor were his troubles at an end.

Retaining his hold, Bunduki stepped over the supine *Bul-Mok* and rolled him on to his stomach. Before the winded *Mangani* recovered his breath or scattered wits, his captor had dropped to ram both knees on to the base of his spine. Having done so, Bunduki transferred his hands and cupped them under *Bul-Mok's* chin. Interlacing his fingers, he drew the head back and forced downwards with his knees.

Massive muscles bulged and writhed as the blond giant bent his victim's spine in an agonizing and dangerous fashion. Half-strangled, winded and partially dazed, *Bul-Mok* could do no more than beat his fists futilely on the ground in a frenzy of pain.

Even as Bunduki started to apply what would have been the final, fatal pressure, he once more had the sensation of being watched. Not just by the other occupants of the clearing either, although they were taking a considerable interest in what was going on. The scrutiny seemed to be originating elsewhere, possibly from among the trees that encircled the clearing, but he refused to permit it to distract him. Instead of trying to locate the unknown observers, he concentrated his attention on matters closer at hand.

Showing an ever-increasing excitement, the three young males—particularly *Bal-Tak*—watched their father's predicament. Squealing and grunting without the sounds forming understandable words, they jumped up and down like excited gorillas or chimpanzees. Despite that, they kept their distance. There could, they all realized, be no intervention in such a conflict. As *Bul-mok* had clearly accepted the strange-looking white creature as a *Mangani,* it must be settled between the two participants.

The younger brothers were merely restive and excited, but *Bal-Tak* had an even deeper interest. Being second in the line of the hierarchy, he could recognize the threat to his status and position. If the strange white skin, who clearly knew the ways of the *Mangani,* defeated *Bul-Mok*—which now seemed very likely—he could assume command of the family. That would mean he became the dominant male whom *Bal-Tak* must eventually challenge and overthrow to assume command.

Although possessing less than a human being's powers of reasoning, *Bal-Tak's* sentience warned him that, being younger, *Tar-Ara* would be much more difficult than *Bul-Mok* to depose. Having managed to draw that conclusion, however, his intelligence was insufficient to find a solution. Certainly the thought of going to his father's assistance never occurred to him.

Assuming a kneeling posture, the girl stared at the giant man who had saved her. She feasted her eyes on his handsome face and wonderfully well-developed body, rapidly losing her fear of the "Hairy Men." The fright was being replaced by another, more pleasurable sensation.

Ever since the girl could remember, she had been told stories of a great jungle god who rescued Telonga maidens in distress. Although she had never really believed that such a person existed, for nobody had ever seen him, she now felt compelled to change her mind. The magnificent white-haired giant had certainly come to her aid in a time of greater danger than she had ever previously known. Apart from his light colour, he was assuredly all that she would have expected of a jungle god. No man of her people—not even *At-Vee,* the Hunter—could equal her saviour's handsome features, enormous size and exceptional muscular development.

As the girl recollected what the legends claimed would happen after the maiden was saved, she wriggled her shapely body in ecstatic anticipation. Excitedly and eagerly, she thought of the love making which she felt sure was coming once the jungle god had driven away the "Hairy Men."

With the *Mangani's* spine on the point of breaking, Bunduki refrained from applying the final pressure. He had no wish to kill, or seriously injure—which would most likely have the same result—*Bul-Mok* unless there was no other choice. It was possible that the need to do so would not arise. In all forms of status-conflict between males of the same species, there were ways of bringing the affair to an end without the need to kill the loser. From what Tarzan and Korak had told him, Bunduki knew what he could do to avoid terminating the *Mangani's* life.

"Surrender?" the blond giant demanded, loosening his grip slightly without entirely relinquishing the painful hold.

"Surrender!" *Bul-Mok* conceded, after a moment's pause, knowing that the offer was unlikely to be repeated.

Although each had made the same phonetic word-sound, *"Ka-goda,"* the difference in the timbre of their voices showed that one had asked a question and the other had given an answer.

Separating his hands on receiving *Bul-Mok's* reply, Bunduki leapt to his feet and stood astride his defeated rival's recumbent body. Watched by the girl and the three younger males, he tossed back his head and roared forth the victory call of a bull *Mangani*. There was no immediate response from *Bal-Tak* or his brothers, but somewhere to the north-west came a distant reply and another sounded faintly from the east. That implied there were other bands of *Mangani* in the jungle. However, both groups were much too far away to concern him.

Having signalled his victory in the accepted manner, Bunduki turned his back on the three young males. Smiling and apparently satisfied that he had achieved his purpose, he started to walk towards the kneeling girl.

Letting out a snarl of rage, *Bal-Tak* leapt into motion. He swung the branch-spear above his head in both hands, intending to drive its sharpened end into the unsuspecting blond giant's back.

CHAPTER FOUR

I'll Let You Have Your Revenge

REALIZING that she had no other choice, Dawn Drummond-Clayton came to a halt and turned.

She was not a moment too soon!

In fact, she had almost left it too late!

Already the harpy eagle's broad, shortish wings were lifting it higher, in preparation for the deadly downwards plunge onto its prey. From its powerful curved beak burst a hideous shriek that was intended to paralyse its victim with fright during the final stages of the attack.

Reversing its wing beats and spreading its tail feathers, the eagle inclined its body almost vertically. It thrust the sturdy yellow legs forward, directing the deadly implements with which it made its kill towards its prey. The huge, hooked claws—the ones at the rear not quite as long but thicker than those of a Kodiak bear, the largest carnivorous land animal in the world —opened to a span as great as the hand of a big man. They were ready to drive into and clamp hold of its victim's flesh.

For once, the terror-inducing scream was failing to achieve its purpose. The creature at which it was flying was far more dangerous than the arboreal animals and large jungle birds that formed the eagle's natural prey. Nor was the girl a slave with bound arms, as the other human beings at whom it had been flown invariably were. They had been unable to fight back, but she could.

Adopting her shooting stance, Dawn made ready to

defend herself. While her left hand started to raise the bow, the fingers of her right were manipulating the string and arrow. A draw of twenty-eight inches was required to flex the limbs sufficiently to obtain their full power. Before she had attained a quarter of that distance, she knew there would not be enough time for her to achieve it.

Ever nearer swooped the huge bird. The six-foot-six-inch spread of the broad wings, the width of its breast and the great fan of the rather long, squared-off tail seemed to be blocking out the sky. Its enormous curved talons appeared to be growing bigger as they rushed in the girl's direction.

After having gained no more than seventeen inches of the draw, Dawn did not dare wait any longer. She was aiming by instinctive alignment. However, at such short range, it would be accurate enough for her needs. Unhooking her fingers, she released the straining string.

The arrow was propelled forward, but at far less than the full seventy pounds' pressure.

Would it have gathered sufficient momentum to achieve its purpose?

Across the chasm, the riders were watching with considerable interest and mixed emotions.

Dryaka, High Priest of the Mun-Gatah nation, had been furious when Charole sent her harpy eagle after the girl. Although his original thoughts had been of the libidinous pleasures he would have at the expense of the beautiful stranger after her capture, he had decided that she might serve an even more useful purpose. Clearly she was strong and had claimed to be a warrior. Perhaps she could help him to dispose of the greatest threat to the powerful position which he held among his people.

For her part, Charole had guessed what the High Priest had had in mind when she noticed the change in the way he had been studying the girl across the chasm. Charole could only retain her rights and title of Protectress of the Quagga God as long as no other woman could wrest them from her. Just as she constantly hoped to find a man who would destroy Dryaka for her, so the High Priest was forever seeking a woman capable of deposing her. Knowing that her removal from office was the main reason for Dryaka's desire to see Dawn captured, Charole had been determined that the girl would be seriously injured—or killed—before she fell into their hands.

Having launched the eagle, the Protectress settled comfortably on her saddle. Real cruelty showed on her beautiful face as the bird sped upon its mission and she ignored Dryaka's obvious displeasure at her actions.

There were few of the Mun-Gatah people, brave warriors as many of them undoubtedly were, who would have dared to deliberately incur the High Priest's wrath. However, while Dryaka possessed great power, Charole could claim to be of equal importance. As Protectress of the Quagga God, particularly while she had the active support of three out of the six members of the ruling Council of Elders, she had little to fear from the scowling man by her side. In fact, as long as she held her high office and could claim the backing of sufficient followers, she was virtually the co-ruler of the Mun-Gatah nation.

Watching the eagle swooping towards Dawn, Charole smiled. It had been trained to tackle human beings, although they had up to that point always been bound and helpless slaves. The results had always been highly entertaining and she felt sure that they would be even more so on this occasion. Having seen the terrible damage that the bird could inflict with its talons and beak, she doubted whether the stranger would pose any further threat to her after the completion of the attack.

Realizing that Charole had deduced the real reason for his interest in Dawn, Dryaka was equally aware of the girl's danger. Much as he would have liked to call a warning when Dawn had not appeared to know that the eagle was following her, he had known better than to do so. The balance of power between himself and the Protectress was so even that it might easily be tilted in either's favour. If he had helped a foreigner, especially should she escape as a result of it, he would be placing a powerful lever in his rival's hands. Nor would she be slow in making use of it, As always, the hunting party was comprised of an equal number of his and her supporters. Let him lose control of his adherents' loyalty and he might never again see the Temple of the Quagga God.

With that in mind, Dryaka drew what consolation he could as he saw the girl had become aware of her peril and was turning to meet it. If she could not protect herself, then she lacked the qualities which he required. To handle that unusual, powerful-looking bow would call for strength and skill. If those qualities were matched by fighting prowess—and, apart from the Telonga, most of the nations had their share of women warriors her capture might provide him with the means to remove Charole. When that had been brought about, he would ensure the next Protectress was somebody more amenable to his will. He hoped that Dawn would prove worthy of his confidence.

Dryaka would very soon know the answer!

Holding her breath, Dawn watched the arrow and the diving eagle as they converged and met. Their combined speeds caused the four-blade Bear Razorhead's needle-sharp point to impale the black-plumed breast and its quadruple cutting edges slashed their way through to reach the vital organs.

Almost as soon as the arrow had passed beyond the bow's handle-riser, Dawn flung herself aside. She saw the eagle jerk upon being hit. Screaming in agony, its controlled diving flight turned into a dying plunge earthwards. One wildly flailing wing brushed her shoulder in passing, but she had avoided any serious—or even minor—injury. Swinging around and reaching to pivot an arrow from the bow-quiver, she watched the bird's death throes as it crashed to the ground and felt a touch of sympathetic sorrow for having been the cause of them.

"May the Quagga God stamp you dead, foreign bitch!"

Redolent of feminine hatred and anger, the screamed out words reached Dawn's ears and drew her attention from the magnificent creature that she had been compelled to kill. Nocking the arrow to the bow's string, she swung her gaze to the people on the other side of the chasm. The second group were riding down the slope and, having leapt from his zebra, the eagle's attendant started shaking his fists furiously at the girl.

However, it was the gold-clad beauty and the tall man who were of the most interest to Dawn. The woman was screaming more curses and seemed almost besides herself with rage. Although the girl could not be certain at that distance, she got the impression that the man was pleased by her escape from the eagle.

Cold anger started to surge through Dawn as she listened to some of the vile threats that the woman was shrieking at her. She became filled with an almost uncontrollable desire to silence the other's raging voice by serving her in the same way that she had treated the eagle. Before Dawn could stop herself, she raised and began to draw the bow.

Charole's furious tirade died away as she saw what the girl was doing. Alarm bit at her as she realized just how vulnerable to reprisals she was. The powerful looking bow would propel its arrow at her as easily as the eagle had winged across the chasm and be even more deadly if it struck home.

For a moment Charole was tempted to fling herself from the saddle and hide behind her quagga's body. She restrained the impulse just in time, being aware of how Dryaka's clique and, even more important, her own followers would react to such a display of cowardice. Flickering a glance at the High Priest, she found that he was watching her. The mocking sneer of his face implied that he had noticed her fear and deduced what she had been contemplating. In which case, there was no easy way in which she could avoid the danger.

With the bow in the shooting position and its arrow

almost drawn to the full, reason returned to Dawn. The two riders were drawing closer and every second's delay was decreasing her already slim chances of reaching the woodland. Turning her head, she discovered that they were less than a quarter of a mile away.

Forgetting her intention of taking revenge on the woman who had been reviling her, the girl swung away and resumed her flight. Although she allowed the arrow to slide forward under control, she once again left it in position. She was accepting the difficulty of running like that against the benefit of having it ready for immediate use.

"It *is* a pity that your eagle failed to stop her, Charole," Dryaka remarked, in tones of mock commiseration. "If you wish, I'll let you have your revenge when Tomlu catches her."

"That is *kind* of you," the Protectress answered, with a poison-sweet politeness. "And when Ragbuf brings her to me, I'll let you have her—after *I've* finished with her."

Neither Charole nor Dryaka would willingly allow their respective factions to become the weaker, so each had sent one man to scout for game across the river. Whichever reached the departing girl first would be able to claim her for his leader.

Having heard the brief exchange of comments, the six riders from the ridge separated into their two factions. They moved into position behind their leaders and watched the scouts galloping recklessly in pursuit of the foreign girl.

Being fully aware of the rivalry between their leaders, Ragbuf and Tomlu did not need to be told that the Protectress and the High Priest would each want to take the girl for his, or her, own use. So the scouts were mutually determined to be the one who made the capture. Considerably smaller and lighter than his companion, Ragbuf began to draw ahead. Snarling a curse, Tomlu tried ot force more speed out of his zebra.

"What will you do with her, Charole?" asked the woman whose footwear followed the style worn by the

Protectress, throwing a triumphant glance at her opposite number in Dryaka's faction as Ragbuf gained a full length's lead on Tomlu.

Before any reply could be made, Ragbuf's mount dropped its right front hoof into a hole. Screaming with agony as the leg snapped, it went down and pitched its rider over its head. Concentrating on the girl, he was unable to save himself and was catapulted helplessly to the ground. The lance flew from his hand as he made a belated attempt to break his fall. Failing to do so, he landed head first. There was a sharp pop as his neck broke and his body slid onwards for a few feet. Whooping derisively and not offering to stop to see how badly the other man was injured, Tomlu galloped by.

"You don't seem to have the Quagga God's favour today, Charole," commented the sultry, beautiful brunette from her place at the High Priest's left side.

"Perhaps *you* would like to see how far He has withdrawn his favour, Elidor?" the Protectress spat back viciously and her right hand crossed to the hilt of her sword.

"Tomlu will soon have her," Elidor said, without meeting Charole's challenging gaze. Instead, as she was not ready to take up the other's offer and yet was equally unwilling to make her refusal obvious, she pretended to be wholly absorbed in the pursuit.

If the Protectress had been less interested in the result of the chase, she might have forced the issue. Elidor was her most prominent rival and Dryaka's choice to be her successor. As yet, they had not clashed but Charole knew that it was only a matter of time before they must. However, she intended to be the one who chose when, where and how it took place. Believing herself to be the better swordswoman, she was determined that they would be the weapons selected when the confrontation happened. For the moment, she decided to forego the opportunity and continued to stare across the chasm.

Hearing the scream of the zebra, followed by the crashes as it and its rider struck the ground, Dawn threw a glance over her shoulder. One of her pursuers was down, but the other showed no sign of stopping to help him.

Striding along as fast as her legs would carry her, the girl accepted that she could not hope to reach the trees. Nor, if she kept running at that pace, would she be in any condition to defend herself should the need arise—which it was practically certain to do.

With her bosom heaving and straining at the dress's fastenings as she sought to replenish her lungs, Dawn halted and turned towards her pursuer. He was big, burly, very muscular and had a surly, brutal face. Even with the extensive knowledge of various forms of un-armed combat acquired during her formative tomboy years and never forgotten, she doubted whether she could fight him off with her bare hands. Nor was she enamoured with the idea of using her knife.

That left her with the Ben Pearson Marauder bow and its fiber glass arrows.

Dawn felt considerable qualms about the possibility of having to take another human being's life. Watching the man galloping closer, she forced herself to accept that she might not have any other choice. Nothing in his attitude, particularly the way in which he had ignored his fallen companion, suggested that he might be disposed towards mercy and compassion. In fact, his whole demeanour implied exactly the opposite. If his expression was any guide, he was already savouring the pleasures which he felt sure would be his after he had made her a captive.

At that moment, the girl started to experience a sen-sation similar to one she had felt when competing be-fore spectators in some athletic event. She was being watched and not just by the burly pursuer, or even the rest of his party beyond the chasm. Yet the man gave no indication of being aware of the mysterious observ-ers. Nor had Dawn seen anything of them during her flight. Concluding, from the way they were keeping themselves concealed, that she could not count on them to help her she knew that she must deal with the man unaided.

Lifting the butt of his lance from the socket on the stirrup, Tomlu turned it forward instead of to the rear. Although he had not received any advice or instructions, he knew that Dryaka would want the girl taken alive and with as little permanent injury as possible. That was understandable. The people preferred active sacrifices for the Quagga God, such being more entertaining to watch as the victims tried to escape or to make a fight to save their lives. While a blow to the stomach with the butt of the lance would render her helpless for long enough to let him secure her, it would not seriously incapacitate her.

Grimly setting her teeth, Dawn started to raise the bow. While doing so, she did her best to control her heavy breathing. The way it was causing her chest to heave, she could not hope to do any accurate shooting. In fact, it might even seriously impede her ability to handle the far from inconsiderable draw weight of the powerful hunting bow.

Being aware of the problems, the girl watched the approaching rider. She sensed that she could not expect to bluff or intimidate the burly man, but hoped he might recognize the danger and keep his distance.

The hope did not materialize!

The man was continuing to ride straight at her!

Leaning sideways at an angle of almost forty-five degrees on the saddle of his well-trained zebra, Tomlu was studying his potential victim. He watched her presenting her weapon at him, but did not feel unduly alarmed. An experienced warrior, he had come into contact with archers on several occasions and was satisfied that he knew their limitations.

The girl, Tomlu noticed, was showing signs of having run both fast and far since killing Charole's eagle. What was more, as she began to draw the bow, he observed with satisfaction that she was taking the easiest target and aiming at the centre of his broad chest. That reduced the danger to him and he was grateful that she was not making his mount her target. No arrow, even when discharged by a man, had contrived to pierce his breastplate of one and a half inch thick, sun-dried and specially hardened rhinoceros hide.* So he believed, with some justification in the light of past events, that he had nothing to fear from a woman.

While she was drawing back the arrow towards its anchor point, Dawn was all too conscious of the way in which it was moving in concert with the rising and falling of her bosom. Try as she might, she could not keep the weapon steady.

Dawn realized that, in a very short time, the man would be in striking distance. Nor did she draw any erroneous conclusions from the way he was holding the lance. Its butt would prove as effective as the point of it should make contact. Even more so, if—as she suspected—it was his intention to take her alive.

Forcing herself to remain calm and striving desperately to control her breathing, the girl finally yielded to the inevitable. There was, she realized, no hope of the man turning away. For all that, she still hesitated. If she should miss with the arrow, she was all too aware that she would not have sufficient time to extract a replacement, even from the more readily accessible bow-quiver, nock, draw, take aim and loose it at her assailant.

*The immunity offered against archers by their breastplates was the reason why the Mun-Gatah nation had never bothered to make use of bows and arrows, even for hunting. The shields of the Masai in Kenya gave a similar protection from Wa-Kamba or Kikuyu bowmen so they too took no interest in archery as a means of defense and attack.

CHAPTER FIVE

If You Follow, Tar-Ara Kill!

"LOOK behind you!" the brown-skinned girl screamed, pointing a finger in the hope that it would help to explain what she meant if the "jungle god" did not understand the Telonga language.

Awe, reverence—and something more earthy—had come to the girl's pretty and expressive face as, having watched her rescuer deal with *Bul-Mok* and turn in her direction, she had started to rise. However, seeing the second of the "Hairy Men" commencing an attack on the blond giant—who did not appear to appreciate the danger his incautious behaviour had created—she was determined to alert him to it. Once he had extricated himself from the predicament, which she felt sure he could do, he would be suitably grateful for the warning.

The girl's words had not been necessary, even though—in some mysterious way—Bunduki had been able to understand them. He had known there was nothing more to fear from *Bul-Mok* after having received the surrender, but he intended to establish a similar sense of inferiority upon the rest of the bulls. If there was to be a further challenge, he had known it would come from the second largest male.

Glancing at *Bal-Tak* after having given his victory roar, the blond giant had guessed that he was building up his courage but was not quite ready to make his move. That was why Bunduki had turned his back on the three young bulls. He was hoping that his disdainful attitude would goad *Bal-Tak* into trying to take advantage of the opportunity and attack. So he had been alert for the first hint that he had succeeded.

Having heard the *Mangani's* growl and the sound of his approaching feet, Bunduki was already starting to turn as the words were leaving the girl's lips.

"*Bal-Tak* kill!" the young *Mangani* bellowed, despite his surprise at seeing his intended victim swinging to face him.

Roaring out the threat, despite an inclination to retreat from his obviously prepared foe, *Bal-Tak* continued to rush forward. Instead of following what would have been the most sensible course and retreating, he raised and prepared to deliver a powerful downwards thrust with his branch-spear when he came within striking distance.

The young bull was not allowed to complete his proposed attack.

Thinking and moving at a much faster speed than the *Mangani* was capable of, Bunduki sprang at him. Out drove the blond giant's clenched right fist. It ploughed with terrible force into *Bal-Tak's* solar plexus before he could bring down the spear. Halted in his tracks by the power of the blow, the *Mangani* acted as a human being would under the circumstances. Letting go of his branch-spear, he folded over at the waist and his hands flew to the point of impact in an instinctive, if futile, attempt to lessen the suffering he was experiencing.

Stepping forward a pace and pivoting on his right foot to gain extra impetus, Bunduki swung and propelled his left knee upward. It caught the *Mangani* in the centre of the chest. Lifted erect and from his feet by the impact, *Bal-Tak* pitched over to land winded and helpless on his back.

"*Ka—Ka-goda!*" *Bal-Tak* managed to gasp out as his assailant loomed above him.

Accepting the surrender, Bunduki went by his fallen foe. He wanted to complete the establishment of his superiority over the other two young males. From the perturbed way they were watching him approach, he did not anticipate any great difficulty in doing so.

"You fight?" Bunduki demanded, glaring at the third largest bull.

"No!" was the immediate reply, followed by a rapid retreat for several feet.

Without even waiting to be challenged, the smallest of the quartet dropped his branch-spear and scuttled away.

Satisfied that he had attained an absolute moral and physical ascendancy over the *Mangani,* at least for the time being, the blond giant once more turned and went towards the girl. He glanced at *Bul-Mok* and *Bal-Tak* in passing. Although the former had risen, he slunk away holding his back with one hand and avoided meeting Bunduki's eyes. The latter was sitting up in a painful manner and was too concerned with his woeful feelings to even look at the man who had caused them.

It was Bunduki's intention to retrieve his bow and then question the girl. Before he could do either, she flung herself into his arms. Once there, she clung hold and wriggled her warm, almost naked and very curvaceous body in a way that suggested relief over her escape was not her only reason for coming so close.

"Don't be afraid," Bunduki said, guessing that he was speaking a language she could understand. He removed her arms from around his neck and eased her gently away. "They won't harm you now."

"I am not afraid now that I'm with you, great god of the jungle," the girl replied, attempting to come close but held beyond her arms' length by his hands on her shoulders. "I am Joar-Fane. Do you like me?"

" 'The Loving One,' " the blond giant translated silently, keeping the girl at a distance. "I bet you live up to it." Aloud, he went on, "Where do you live, I will take you there."

Even as Bunduki made the offer, he realized that carrying it out might delay his search for Dawn. The *Manganis'* attitudes had suggested that they had had little or no contact with human begins. So the girl's home would probably be a long way off.

A disappointed frown came to Joar-Fane's features. When a woman was rescued by a jungle god, she did not expect him to be in such a hurry to return her to her village. Perhaps he required a hint to assure him of her feelings.

"I don't know where it is and I don't care," the girl stated with a toss of her head. "I will stay with you, jungle god. I'll make you a fine wife, you'll see."

Still holding Joar-Fane away from him, Bunduki wondered what he could do with her. If he tried to locate her village, she might deliberately mislead him. Or she could really be lost and have no idea of the direction in which her home was situated. In either event, he would be delayed—possibly for days—in his attempt to find Dawn. That was something which he did not care to contemplate. He had seen sufficient to realize that the jungle contained many perils, some of which—such as the presence of *Mangani*—were different from anything she might be expecting.

"What is your name, great god of the jungle?" Joar-Fane continued, when her words failed to elicit the desired response.

"Bunduki," the blond giant replied, being able to say his name while speaking the girl's language although it had been impossible when using the much more primitive speech of the *Manganis*. "But I'm not a god. I'm just a man."

"Bunduki," Joar-Fane repeated, speaking the word slowly. Then she returned on her most winning smile. "Bunduki. *Bunduki*. I like it. I've never seen such a beautiful man as you, Bunduki, and I'll make you a very fine wi———."

Hoping to chill the girl's ardour by a display of indifference, the blond giant pushed her gently aside. Her words had been trailing away even before he did so, and she was staring past him in an alarmed fashion. He swung around, wanting to find out what had attraced—or diverted—her attention.

Several more *Mangani* were coming from the game trail. There were five females; one big and old, the others younger but fully developed. A dozen children of various ages were trailing along and two immature bulls brought up the rear. Joining the newcomers, the two youngest members of the first party started to explain—as well as their limited vocabulary would allow —what had happened. The females and the youngsters did not listen with any great display of interest. In fact, long before the explanations were completed, they were beginning to scatter and forage for food in the bushes and grass at the edge of the clearing.

Bunduki decided that it might be advisable to leave. There was a chance that the presence of *Bul-Mok's* family would arouse his protective instincts and cause him to lead a mass attack by the other bulls.

Gathering up his bow, the blond giant went to retrieve the arrow from *Bul-Mok's* ruined club. If his suspicions regarding the jungle were correct, it would be impossible for him to obtain replacements of such quality and materials. The girl scuttled after him, darting frightened glances at the *Mangani*. Having advanced with the intention of attempting to reach the dead capybara, the largest of the young females gave a snarl and rushed towards Joar-Fane.

"Back!" Bunduki roared, reverting to *Mangani* and placing himself between the girl and the female.

Ignoring the command, the she-*Mangani* continued to advance. The big blond did not hesitate in his response. Stepping forward and dropping the club with the arrow still in it, he delivered a right hand cuff to the side of the disobedient female's head that was hard enough to knock her sprawling. After that, none of the others tried to come near and, on regaining her feet, the first one hurried away.

Handing his bow to Joar-Fane who was staring at him with an expression that—under the circumstances —he found disconcerting, Bunduki picked up the club and drew free his arrow. Tossing the club aside, he led the way to the capybara he had killed. Looking at it, the girl let out a gasp.

"No Telonga could have done this!" the girl declared, indicating the arrow which had sunk to cresting* so that its head had emerged on the other side. Then another, more pressing thought diverted her and she ran the tip of her tongue across her full red lips. "The water-pig is good meat. Even a wild one."

"Are you hungry?" Bunduki inquired, looking at her as he was kneeling by the carcass.

"I have not eaten more than berries and fruit since I escaped from the Mun-Gatahs' People-Taker three days ago," Joar-Fane replied.

"Who is he?" Bunduki asked, removing the broadhead from the adapter on the bluff-coloured arrow's shaft.

"He comes to our villages with his men and women and takes the people."

"Don't your men stop them?"

"The hunters sometimes say they should, but the Elders put them away before the People-Taker comes so there won't be any trouble," Joar-Fane explained. "I don't know what happens to those who are taken. None of them have ever come back."

"You say that you escaped," the blond giant prompted, drawing the headless arrow free from the capybara and standing up. "Did anybody come after you?"

"Three of his men and a woman," the girl replied.

"Where are they now?"

"I don't know. They followed me across the Big River after I had fallen in, but I haven't seen them to-day."

Although Bunduki was interested in the girl's story, he decided that they would postpone continuing with it until they had crossed the stream and left the *Mangani* behind. So, having fitted the head back on the

*Cresting: the bands of colour painted for the purpose of identification around the arrow's shaft just in front of the fletching.

shaft, he returned the arrow to the quiver and swung it across his back. Taking the bowie knife from its sheath, he used it to sever a hind leg from the capybara.

"This ought to be enough meat for us," he told the girl as he cleaned the blade of the knife with a handful of grass. Sheathing it, he went on, "If we leave the rest for the 'Hairy People,' they won't trouble us."

"Very well, Bunduki," Joar-Fane assented. "I'll carry the meat."

"There is food," the blond giant announced in *Mangani,* indicating the remains of his prey. "We go. If you follow, *Tar-Ara* kill!"

Having delivered the warning, Bunduki took his bow from the girl and strode towards the stream. Collecting the bloody leg, she glided after him. There was pride in her sensual, graceful posture and she darted a triumphant glance at the big female who had attempted to attack her. Seeing the other bare her teeth, Joar-Fane hurried to the blond giant's side. Although encumbered by their meat, she attempted to take hold of his empty right hand. He avoided being trapped and, after a warning that he wanted the hand free in case they should be attacked, she desisted.

With its bed consisting of firm, clean gravel and a depth of no more than three feet, the stream presented no difficulty for the girl or Bunduki. Its waters were clear and the current mild, allowing him to make sure there were no dangerous creatures or fish.

"Shall we take off our clothes and let them dry?" Joar-Fane inquired hopefully as they reached the opposite bank and walked ashore.

"No," Bunduki said, hiding the grin which was caused by knowing what prompted the suggestion. "We'll keep going. The sun will dry them."

Ignoring the girl's disappointed pout, the big blond looked back across the stream. The *Mangani* were eagerly approaching his kill. Moving stiffly, *Bul-Mok* let out a furious bellow as one of the younger males tried to precede him. Although his son backed away,

Bunduki guessed that the dominant bull would have to reassert his ascendancy after suffering his defeat.

"Where do you live, Joar-Fane?" the blond giant asked, putting the *Mangani* from his thoughts and starting to walk towards the north-west.

"Beyond the Big River," the girl replied vaguely, trotting at his side.

"Where is that?"

"I don't know."

Striding along, Bunduki looked down at the girl and silently admitted that she might be speaking the truth. In the jungle it was too easy for an inexperienced person to lose all sense of direction. That did nothing to reduce his predicament. He did not want to postpone his search for Dawn while trying to return Joar-Fane to her village. So, he concluded, he must take the little girl with him. Once they had found his adoptive cousin, the pair of them could escort Joar-Fane to her home.

"Something tells me that I might need a chaperone," the big blond mused, glancing at the pretty girl as her hot little hand closed on his. "Or a bodyguard might be better."

Allowing Joar-Fane to retain her grip, much to her delight and satisfaction, Bunduki guided her through the jungle. The warmth of the sun soon dried their garments, as he had said it would.

Although the girl claimed that the area through which they were passing had always been notorious for the numbers and ferocity of the "Hairy People" who occupied it, they neither saw nor heard any more of the *Mangani*. There were plenty of other creatures, but nothing that posed a threat to their safety even though Joar-Fane behaved in a frightened manner no matter how harmless a beast they saw. After a short time, Bunduki suspected that her behaviour was merely an excuse to nestle up to him.

From her comments, the girl clearly knew little about animals. In fact, she confessed that she had very rarely left her village. When forced to make a journey it had always been accompanied by older people. They had stuck to clearly marked trails and never ventured into the jungles.

There was, however, little conversation as they walked along. While Bunduki would have liked to learn more about the land in which he found himself, the girl had something *very* different in mind as a topic of conversation. It was one which did not meet with his approval under the circumstances. So he instructed her to keep quiet until they stopped for a rest. When she began to protest he warned her that some wild beast or the "Hairy People" might stalk them and take them by surprise unless he could hear and prevent it. The ruse served its purpose. She stopped her chatter, but continued to cling to his hand and stare nervously about her.

After they had covered about six miles, Bunduki was satisfied that *Bul-Mok* and his family were not following them. They were descending into a wide valley, through which ran a small stream.

"I'm hungry and tired," Joar-Fane hinted, breaking her silence.

"Then we'll eat and rest," Bunduki answered.

Hurrying to the banks of the stream, Joar-Fane set down the capybara's leg and knelt to drink. She was genuinely tired and hungry, but had another idea in mind when she mentioned the fact. After they had fed and rested, she felt sure that she could persuade her rescuer to take a much greater interest in her than he had been doing so far.

If she could not, the little girl told herself grimly, then she had no right to the name, "The Loving One."

CHAPTER SIX

I Want To Catch That Girl!

"TOMLU has her!' Dryaka enthused as he watched his adherent charging towards Dawn Drummond-Clayton. "She'll soon be *mine!*"

Hearing the excited chatter of agreement from the other members of the High Priest's faction, Charole darted a glance filled with disappointment and bitter animosity at him. From the moment that Ragbuf's mount had fallen, she had been aware that Tomlu was almost certain to make the capture. What was more, the way in which he had turned the butt of his lance to the front had warned her that he was intending to take the prisoner alive.

Watching Dawn swing around, raise and start to draw the bow, the Protectress of the Quagga God found herself torn between two conflicting desires. While she would have liked to lay her hands on the beautiful stranger—towards whom she had formed an instant and implacable hatred—she wanted it to be on her own terms. Certainly she did not wish Dryaka to gain the satisfaction and—if, as seemed likely, Dawn should prove an entertaining sacrifice—the acclaim of the population for having brought in such a prisoner.

Charole found herself on the verge of hoping that the girl would escape. However, even though she guessed that the High Priest could read her thoughts, she knew better than to voice them aloud.

Making an effort, Dawn managed to hold her breath. She had the arrow drawn to its anchor point, with the fletching brushing against her cheek. With the man so close and the need for haste, she aimed in the style known as "gap shooting." She concentrated her full attention upon the centre of his chest, although still conscious of, and taking into consideration, the amount of space between the arrow's point and its target. The size of the space, or "gap," became a guide to the angle of elevation that was required and she could if necessary adjust her weapon accordingly.

The necessity did not arise!

In fact, Tomlu was so near by that time that the tip of Dawn's arrow was sighted straight on its intended mark.

He was at her point blank range!

Even as the girl relaxed her fingers, she felt disconcerted by her attacker's attitude. He was leering at her and showing neither fear nor concern for his safety, despite the fact that he could see she was aiming the arrow at him. Either he did not know what a bow was, or for some reason he clearly felt that he was in no danger.

There was no time for Dawn to ponder on the phenomenon. Released from her restraint, the arrow was sent on its way.

Tomlu was still grinning when the missile struck the centre of his breastplate, sent there with the full propulsive power of the bow's draw weight of seventy pounds. Instead of bouncing back, or being deflected, the point passed through the rhinoceros hide as if it was so much wet, soft paper. Shock and amazement mingled with the agony that was distorting the burly man's brutish features as the arrow's quadruple blades cut deeper and deeper into his chest cavity.

While the Mun-Gatah scout had been correct in his estimation of the point at which the girl was aiming, all of his other caclulations had been woefully, completely and fatally wrong. Yet it had been an understandable error, born out of his ignorance of the full facts regarding her weapons.

The archers against whom Tomlu had previously been brought into conflict all used primitive wooden bows of, at most, a forty pounds' draw weight. No all wood "self" bow could match the tensile strength of a unidirectional fiber glass precision implement such as the Ben Pearson Marauder.* That was particularly true when, as was the case with the Mun-Gatahs' usual enemies, it was discharged from a chest draw.

Nor did his previous foes possess arrows to equal those used by the girl. The exceptionally fine temper of the steel used to manufacture the four-blade head was far superior to anything that Tomlu had come across. So, instead of being halted or turned aside by his erstwhile protective breastplate, the girl's shaft had been able to slice through it and into his torso.

Although the burly scout did not remain in error for long regarding his assumptions, the lesson he learned was of no use to him.

An involuntary jerk by the stricken man's left hand caused his fast-moving zebra, trained to be instantly obedient to such signals, to swerve in that direction. With its rider already starting to lose his balance and allowing the lance to slip from his grasp, the alteration toppled him from the saddle. Slipping out of the stirrup-irons, his feet did nothing to help him retain his seat. Falling, he landed on his right shoulder and bounced three times before coming to a halt on his back. It had been such a close thing that Dawn was compelled to leap into the air to avoid being struck by his body.

Turning, the girl started to reach for an arrow from the bow-quiver. While doing so, she dropped her gaze to Tomlu. He lay supine, with the arrow buried almost to its cresting in his chest. There was, she realized, nothing more to be feared from him.

Staring down, Dawn sucked in a long and deep breath as a full understanding of what she had been compelled to do struck her. For a moment she felt close to nausea. Slowly the sensation ebbed away. Com-

---

*The Marauder and other bows of its kind have fiber glass limbs and a wooden handle. Earlier "composite" bows were constructed from layers comprising of combinations of horn, sinew, strips of leather and springy wood.

mon sense told her that here had been no other acceptable course left to her. She was no longer in the civilized world which she had known all her life. Wherever she might be, it was a primitive environment in which a person had to be prepared for defense against human enemies.

The remorse which the girl had started to experience faded away all the more rapidly as she recollected the events that had preceded the killing. Her assailant had meant to capture her and that might, probably would, have resulted in a fate worse than death. Even if he had not raped her, she did not doubt that she would have been badly treated by his companions; particularly the beautiful owner of the harpy eagle. So Dawn considered that she had been completely justified in protecting herself, even to the extent of taking her assailant's life.

Lifting her eyes from the dead man, Dawn turned her attention to his companions on the other side of the chasm. They seemed to have formed into two distinct groups behind the tall man and the gold-clad beauty. All of them appeared to be interested and perturbed by what they had seen. However, the girl had run so far before halting to deal with her remaining pursuer that she could not hear what was being said.

As Dawn suspected, the death of Tomlu had caused considerable consternation among the rest of the Mun-Gatah hunting party. They had shared his confidence in the immunity from the arrow offered by his breastplate. So none of them had been expecting his death.

"Wh—!" Charole gasped, watching Tomlu sliding sideways from the fast-moving zebra. "What's happened?"

None of the others replied, for the very good reason that they were all as surprised as the Protectress and were asking each other similar questions. Also they were all staring at Dawn as she leaped over the scout's body which was bouncing along the ground. The zebra galloped by her.

"She killed him!" Elidor gasped, watching the foreign girl jump and turn. "Lord Dryaka, she *killed* him!"

"But how could she?" asked Sabart, Charole's half-sister and supporter. "He must have fallen off. Or his *grar-gatah** threw him when it swerved."

"Fallen off!" Elidor snorted, more because the statement had been made by a member of the rival faction than out of any respect for Tomlu's capabilities. Being a *banar-gatah* rider herself, she would normally have regarded him as a social inferior and beneath her support. "He's never been *knocked* off, much less *fallen* or been *thrown*. I tell you that she killed him with her bow. Didn't she, my lord?"

"She certainly hit him with it," Dryaka confirmed, automatically corroborating one of his adherents against a follower and kinswoman of the Protectress.

Even as the High Priest was speaking, he began to realize the full implications of what he was saying. A skilled warrior in his own right, he had ridden against and watched Tomlu taking part in training sessions or competitive jousts with the lance. So he could visualize the scout's method and posture during his attack upon the dismounted and, apparently, not too dangerous enemy who was to be captured alive.

Leaning sideways, so as to make a thrust downwards with the lance, Tomlu would have presented only his head, torso, right arm and leg to the foreign girl. Being an experienced fighting man, he would not have offered himself in such a way unless he had felt confident he

---

*Being dwellers on the open plains, the Mun-Gatah people were dependent upon their domesticated zebras to such an extent that their whole culture was based upon the different sub-species of *Equus Quagga* that they bred. The lowest social order rode the *grar-gatah*, which had the striping of a Grant's zebra. People of the next grade had the *ocha-gatah*, with the orange and black stripes of the Burchell's. While the aristocracy made use of the *banar-gatah*, that had been developed from the larger Grevy's. Only the six members of the Council of Elders, the High Priest and the Protectress of the Quagga God had the right to ride a quagga; its name being onomatopoeic and derived from the animal's snort of alarm.

could do so in comparative safety. Which meant he had believed Dawn would miss, or that her arrow was going to strike something upon which it would have no effect. There was only one part of his body that he would regard in that light.

Unless Dawn had been aware of how futile such an action would be and had changed her target at the last moment, giving the scout no indication of her intentions until it was too late for him to counter the motion, she must have been aiming at his chest. So, unless she had sent the arrow into his head, it must have struck and *penetrated* his breastplate.

Dryaka found the latter prospect both disconcerting and alarming, particularly in view of the grandiose plans which he was formulating. The superiority that the Mun-Gatah had over their neighbours was founded in the main upon the protection given by their breastplates. So, if Dawn's nation—whoever they might—be—had a weapon that was capable of penetrating the erstwhile inviolate garments, they would be very dangerous enemies and a serious threat to his scheme.

"Come on!" the High Priest barked, his normally harsh tones made even sharper by the urgency of the situation.

"Where are you going?" Charole inquired, noticing his agitation.

"Across the river," Dryaka answered setting his mount into motion and turning it upstream. "I want to catch that girl!"

Starting her quagga moving, Charole rode alongside the High Priest and covertly studied him. However, she was drawing the wrong conclusions regarding his motives for pursuit. While he still wanted to take Dawn prisoner and use her in a bid to depose the Protectress, he was now more interested in learning the full potential of her bow and arrows.

The rest of the party set off after their leaders. Giving a last furious shake of his fist at the girl, the eagle's attendant vaulted astride his *grar-gatah* and followed.

Watching the riders, Dawn guessed what they had in

mind and knew that the danger from them might not yet be over. The man had told her that the river could be forded above the chasm, which suggested they were intending to cross there and take up the chase themselves.

Having reached that decision, Dawn directed her thoughts towards escaping. From what she had seen from the edge of the chasm, the crossing place was not too close. So she ought to be able to reach the woodland before they arrived on her side of the river. However, while they were showing no indication of taking precautions against her, they might send one of their number to a point of vantage and keep her under observation until the others were over. There was nothing she could do about it if they did and so she must take her chances on outdistancing them.

Deciding that there would not be time to retrieve the arrows which she had expended—in Tomlu's case, she felt disinclined even to try—the girl swung on her heel. Being a skilled horsewoman, she had hoped that she might be able to make use of the man's zebra to carry her away more swiftly than on foot, but it had kept running after losing its rider and there was no hope of catching it.

Setting off at a fast walk, Dawn found herself wondering where Bunduki might be. With him at her side, she would have little to fear from the zebra-riders.

Was her adopted cousin feeling as lonely as she was, finding himself in this strange land and confronted by such inexplicable circumstances?

What conclusions had Bunduki drawn regarding their whereabouts and the means which had brought them there?

Had he too made contact with inhabitants of the strange, alien land?

Thinking about the blond giant was helping to divert Dawn's mind from the memory of Tomlu's evil face as the arrow had driven into his chest.

Keeping moving, Dawn threw several glances towards the chasm. To her relief, all of the riders had gone upstream. They were not making any especial efforts to keep her under observation. Of course, providing that they were capable of doing so, they could follow her tracks. That was highly likely, as tracking was an art in which most primitive people had considerable proficiency. Being experienced in such matters, she realized that she would be travelling faster, even on foot, than they could read the signs which she was making. What was more, if the woodland proved to be suitable, she could take to the trees and avoid leaving traces of her passing on the ground.

On the fringe of the woodland, Dawn paused and studied the land which she had just traversed. Although circling vultures marked the spot, she could no longer see the area around the chasm. Nor, apart from the inevitable wild animals, was there any sign of life along her back trail.

Suddenly, Dawn heard something which drove all thoughts of pursuit from her mind.

Faintly, from a long way off, rose the challenge roar of a bull *Mangani* as he warned others of his kind to stay away from his territory.

For a moment Dawn felt excitement and relief. However, just as she was on the point of replying, a sobering thought struck her.

The call had originated from much too far away for her to identify its maker. There was a possibility that it had been Bunduki, trying to locate her. Yet there was also another alternative. The *Mangani* were extinct in every part of Africa which her family had searched for them, but some might have survived in the unknown jungle beyond the open woodland that she was on the point of entering.

So Dawn kept quiet, knowing that it would be unwise to announce her presence until she was sure of whom she was calling. Instead, she would continue to follow her instincts and keeping going in the direction in which they guided her. Not until she was certain that it was Bunduki giving the challenge would she respond.

Directing a final glance across the plains, without seeing any sign of pursuit, the girl resumed her journey to the south-east. At first, she retained the arrow on the bow's string. Then, feeling hungry and having neither seen nor heard anything to alarm her, she replaced it on the bow-quiver. Laying down the bow, she removed the shoulder-quiver. She had put the remains of the *pemmican* and *biltong* in the pouch of the quiver. Opening it, she reached inside.

Before Dawn could extract the meal, a movement caught the corner of her eye and caused her to look in its direction.

Gripping a spear ready for use, a tall, muscular brown-skinned man clad in a jaguarskin loincloth stepped from behind a tree and confronted her.

CHAPTER SEVEN

What Kind Of Wood Is This?

ALTHOUGH they could not see each other due to the intervening terrain, at about the time that Dawn Drummond-Clayton reached the edge of the woodland, Dryaka, High Priest of the Mun-Gatah—which meant the Riders of the Zebras—nation, was leading his hunting party over the ridge upon which Tomlu and Ragbuf had made their appearances.

Having glided to the ground on almost motionless wings, several vultures were assembling around the two human bodies and the crippled zebra. Attracted in their uncannily efficient manner, a number of spotted hyenas had come loping up. Ignoring the corpses, they made for the injured animal as it tried desperately to rise and escape their attentions.

Although the winged scavengers were as yet too cautious to go any closer, not being sure that the two motionless figures really were dead, they would soon have summoned sufficient courage to commence their gruesome, but necessary, work. However, before they could do so, the appearance of Dryaka's party sent them back into the air and caused the hyenas to make a hurried withdrawal.

The division between the two factions was more marked than it had been when Dawn had last seen them. Talking as they rode upstream, the High Priest complained that it was bad luck that the girl had seen the scouts approaching while they were still so far away. Immediately, Elidor stated that Dawn would not have known they were there but for Sabart having

82

pointed to them thus, warning her of their presence. That had almost caused a physical confrontation between the buxom and pretty Sabart and her accuser. Although he was confident that Elidor could defeat Sabart, Dryaka had used his authority to prevent a fight. He was so determined to capture Dawn that he had not wanted to be delayed while the women settled their disagreement, particularly as the fight could have become general.

Having shared the High Priest's summation regarding the result of a duel between her half-sister and his adherent, Charole had also been willing for it to be averted. She too was very eager to catch Dawn. Having lost face by the death of her eagle, the only way she could regain it was by extracting revenge on the girl.

There was, however, more to it than that. The Protectress was intrigued at the interest shown by Dryaka in going after the girl. While she suspected that he wanted to use Dawn as a means of deposing her, she also believed that there was some other, even more compelling motive. It was, she felt sure, to do with Tomlu's death.

When Charole raised the matter, the High Priest claimed that he wanted to obtain a worthy sacrifice for the Quagga God. She did not believe him. That was the duty of the People-Taker, or—as very few of the Telongas he brought in were suitable for sacrificial purposes—the raiding parties who were sent to collect victims from the more warlike nations and, as such, the task was beneath the dignity of his high office.

Nor was Charole inclined to accept Dryaka's other reason, that he wished to avenge the deaths of the two scouts. The social distinctions of the Mun-Gatah were long established and rigidly enforced. Neither of the men had been even *ocha-gatah* riders, so he was hardly likely to put himself to any great inconvenience on their account.

If anything, the unacceptable excuses served to increase her suspicions. She felt even more certain that his interest went beyond obtaining a challenger who would justify his confidence. To her way of thinking, anything to which the High Priest attached so much importance was worth learning. She might be able to turn it to her advantage. So she had added her support to keeping the peace between the two women.

For all their mutual desire to hunt the girl down, neither the Protectress nor the High Priest would weaken their factions by leaving a member to keep watch and see which direction she was taking as she fled. Nor, in case she had told them the truth about having friends in the vicinity, had they been inclined to reduce their force as a whole by each supplying an observer. They had realized that the omission might lessen their chances of catching Dawn, but neither would yield on the matter.

Bringing his high-spirited, seventeen hand quagga stallion to a halt, Dryaka scanned the expanse of the plains around him. His cold, but very keen eyes located every detail except the one which he had hoped —yet had not really expected—to see. A low snort of disappointment and annoyance burst from him. It was as he had feared. The beautiful stranger had already disappeared.

When last seen, the girl had given the impression that she was making for the woodland. However, he had already discarded the idea of going there by the most direct route. It was possible that she had turned aside before arriving at the trees. In which case, going there could cause them to miss her trail.

The question was, would Dawn take the chance of entering the woodland?

The fact that the girl had been on foot suggested she belonged to a nation who made their home in such terrain, or even in the dense jungle that lay beyond it. If such was the case, she would have a decided advantage over his party while they were all moving among the trees and bushes of the woodland. While they were skilled hunters and excellent trackers, the Mun-Gatahs preferred to seek their prey from the backs of their zebras. That was always difficult in woodland and frequently impossible in the jungle.

However, having given much thought to the matter as he was riding along, the High Priest believed they might find the girl in the savannah rather than the woodland proper or the jungle. The area towards which she had been heading when last seen was inhabited by the brutish, sub-human "Hairy Men." From what he had seen of their ferocity when occasional specimens had been brought in by raiding parties, he doubted whether the girl would dare to enter their domain. She was, in his opinion, more likely to remain in the type of country which the "Hairy Men" usually avoided.

Not that Dryaka had mentioned his conclusions to the others. He would only do so when he could be reasonably sure they were correct. He had a reputation for being right more often than wrong and for rarely making mistakes. It was most useful in retaining the loyalty of his adherents. So, keeping quiet, he turned his attention to try and solve a point which had arisen during the course of his theorizing. It was one that, if he could produce the answer, might supply a clue to the direction Dawn would have to take if she was returning to her homeland.

To which nation did the beautiful, tawny-haired girl belong?

At his first sight of Dawn, Dryaka had thought that she might be an Amazon. Her hair and light-coloured skin had suggested she could be a warrior of that race, but her clothing and armament had been against it. From what he had remembered about the Amazons, those who wore the skins of antelope—being swift-running messengers—were invariably slender. Women who were of Dawn's build and heavier were clad in the skins of a black panther, leopard, lion or tiger. What was more, whether armed with a spear and shield, war-axe or bow, they always carried a sword to augment their knives. No Amazon archer he had ever seen had possessed a bow of the kind so ably wielded by the girl. In fact, he had never come across such a weapon in all his dealings with members of other nations.

Thinking about Dawn's reply when she had been questioned about her origins got the High Priest nowhere. Unknowingly, she had said the word "Apes" in English instead of translating it as "Hairy Men." Naturally, Dryaka had never heard of a nation called the "Apes." Whoever they were, and wherever they made their homes, he told himself, their "Supplier" had given them very special kind of archery equipment.

Even before Tomlu's death, the girl's bow had been a source of interest and speculation to Dryaka. He had been a soldier, raider, temple-guard and People-Taker before attaining his present high office and he had recognized it as something out of the ordinary. If his suspicion about how the scout had been killed was correct, it was definitely an unusual, even remarkable weapon.

Although Dryaka had no intention of letting Charole know, the bow was now his main reason for desiring to make the girl his prisoner.

"Finding her won't be easy," Dryaka warned, at the end of his scrutiny.

"We won't do it by sitting here," Charole answered, impatient as always, moving restlessly on the saddle of her equally large and fine-looking mount.

"Where do you think you're going?" Dryaka challenged, as the Protectress set her quagga into motion.

"After her, of course."

"Where do you intend to start looking?"

Always wary when dealing with the High Priest, Charole read a warning in the tone of his voice. It implied that she was on the point of making a mistake. There must be some fault in her line of reasoning, but she failed to see what it might be. If she went ahead and they should not capture the foreign girl, which she realized was quite likely, Dryaka would claim it was her error of judgment that caused their failure. To have that happen would add to her loss of face over the eagle and might seriously weaken her position by causing the waverers among the population to turn in the High Priest's favour. So, much as it went against the grain, she knew what must be done. However, she saw a way in which she might be able to make the High Priest responsible if things went wrong.

"Where do *you* say we should start looking?" the Protectress inquired, halting her mount and turning her head.

"We'll go to Tomlu's body, then find and follow her tracks from there," Dryaka replied without hesitation. Having seen the trap that had been set for him, he went on, "Even then, we may not catch her. But we may as well try."

Although Charole would have bitten off her tongue rather than have said so, she silently conceded that the High Priest had given sound advice. Going directly to the woodland, as she had intended, without knowing at least approximately where Dawn had entered would have been futile as it would have made finding her tracks difficult and time consuming if not completely impossible. She also noted bitterly that he had avoided the pitfall which she had intended for him.

Without waiting to discover what Charole thought of his suggestion, Dryaka started his quagga moving. The others followed him in silence. There had been little conversation since the quarrel between Elidor and Sabart had ended. Once they had crossed the river, the whole party were too engrossed in scanning the terrain over which they were riding to speak. While there had been no sign of the foreign girl's cousin and his warriors, they could be in the vicinity. Having seen the girl's arrow kill Tomlu, the Mun-Gatahs had had no desire to let themselves be ambushed by several equally well armed and capable archers. So they had considered that unceasing vigilance was of greater importance than talking.

Coming up to Ragbuf's crippled *grar-gatah,* neither the Protectress nor the High Priest deigned to give it or its lifeless rider a single glance. It was left to one of Charole's male adherents to use his lance and put the

animal out of its misery. Dryaka was dividing his attention between the transfixed eagle and Tomlu's body,
with most of it directed at the latter. Duplicating his
actions, Charole was at first unable to decide what he
expected to see.

"By the Quagga God!" one of the male riders ejaculated, his voice throbbing with something close to superstitious awe. "Her arrow went through his breastplate!"

Even as the comment was being made, Dryaka was
placing over his saddlehorn the loop that was attached
to his lance at its point of balance. With its butt in the
cup of the stirrup, the weapon was suspended and his
hands were free. Swinging to the ground, he flipped
the reins over the quagga's head and allowed them to
dangle. Then he went to kneel alongside the body. The
quagga stood motionless, ground-hitched by the hanging reins as effectively as if he had tied them to an im-
movable object. Oblivious of everything else, Dryaka
studied the shaft that rose from Tomlu's chest.

Apart from the eagle's attendant, who had turned
aside and was riding towards his dead charge, only
Charole had continued to advance after Dryaka—who
had put on a short spurt—dismounted. The rest of the
party came to a halt some feet away. They divided their
attention between keeping watch for possible enemies
and staring at the scout, or rather at the thing which
had killed him. Realizing that she must be missing
something of importance, Charole joined the High
Priest on the ground. Schooling her features into an expression of bored disinterest, she stood and watched
him.

"Look at *this!*" Dryaka could not prevent himself
from saying, after he had studied and felt at the shaft
of the arrow.

"I've seen dead men before," the Protectress sniffed,
with a well simulated air of indifference which she
felt sure would elicit further information.

"But you've *never* seen one who was killed like *this!*"
Dryaka protested, so stung by the woman's attitude

that he said more than he had intended. "Look at how deeply the arrow has penetrated."

Once it had been brought to her attention, Charole understood the full implications of the High Priest's statements and guessed that she had unearthed his main reason for wanting to capture the foreign girl.

Then another thought struck the Protectress, causing a slight shudder which she instantly suppressed. Everything pointed to Dawn being an expert archer, with sufficient skill to have hit her mark across the width of the chasm. She remembered the look of hatred on the girl's face when starting to aim the bow at her and realized that she had been *very* close to death at that moment. Without the protection of a leather breastplate, or possibly even if she had had one, Dawn's arrow would have been lethal at the distance which was separating them.

Having no desire to allow the High Priest to see how she was affected by what she saw and thought, the Protectress continued with her pretence of indifference.

"He must have fallen on the arrow and driven it in deeper," Charole commented and pointed to where the attendant was standing glaring at the dead bird. "If her bow was so powerful, it would have sent the arrow straight through my eagle."

"She didn't have time to draw it fully when she loosed it at the bird," Dryaka explained and turned the body on to its side. "Look here! The head has come through the back. No other arrow has ever pierced one of our breastplates, much less gone in this deep and—" he let the corpse go and tapped the nock of the shaft—"there's no dirt here, so he can't have fallen on it."

With that, the High Priest gripped the arrow and tried to withdraw it. Charole was much too interested to comment. Even when he failed to extract the shaft, she remained silent. Opening his hand, he scratched at the cresting with a fingernail and his face took on a deeper, more puzzled frown.

"Fetch me the bird, Elidor!" Dryaka ordered, coming to his feet.

Urging her *banar-gatah* to a gallop, the brunette made her way to where the attendant was crouching over the bird and crooning the Mun-Gatah death chant. She guided the animal in such a way that it was heading straight at the man, causing him to make a hurried leap to the rear to avoid being ridden down. Leaning over without slackening her mount's speed, she bent and scooped up the eagle as she passed. Ignoring the man, who had tripped and was sitting on the ground, she returned to the rest of the party. She brought the zebra to a rump-sliding halt at the High Priest's side and leapt from the saddle almost before its forward motion had ceased. All in all, it had been an excellent piece of riding.

"Here, my lord!" Elidor said and held out the carcass.

Cold anger flickered across Charole's face. She knew that Elidor's behaviour while making the collection was a deliberate affront to her. However, she was too curious about the arrow to take the matter further. Instead, she advanced until she was between the woman and Dryaka. In doing so, she forced Elidor to take a pace to the rear and presented her back to the brunette. She was, nevertheless, confident that her faction would warn her if Elidor made any attempt to take advantage of the opportunity she was offering.

Watching the by-play between the women, the High Priest darted a prohibitive glare at Elidor. Although there was a red flush to her cheeks, she read his meaning correctly. So she kept quiet and stood still.

Plucking the arrow free, Dryaka tossed the dead bird aside. Slowly he rolled the shaft between his fingers, staring intently at it. Then he ran the ball of his left thumb delicately over the tip and cutting edges of the four-bladed point. Having done so, he grasped the shaft at the cresting and just below the point, flexing it to an extent that would have snapped any other arrow he had ever seen.

"What kind of wood is this?" the High Priest said, half to himself, as he felt the arrow's supple strength and watched it return to its former shape when he relaxed his grip. "I've never seen the like of it."

"Let me see," Charole requested and it was indicative of Dryaka's puzzlement that he complied without hesitation. On receiving the arrow, she started to get an inkling of exactly what he meant. However, she could not help yielding to her natural inclination to try and discount any statement made by her rival. "It's just ordinary painted wood."

"Just *ordinary* painted wood?" Dryaka challenged.

"Yes," the Protectress confirmed and, seeing that the rest of the party had moved to positions which allowed them to watch what was going on, she grasped the shaft at each end. Starting to bend it, she continued, "I'll show you."

Much to her amazement, Charole found that the arrow would bend but not break. She heard Elidor's snigger and grimly set her teeth. Laying the shaft across her left thigh, she applied added pressure, but with no greater success. Wild with fury, she jerked out her sword. Taking no notice of the brunette, who backed away a couple of paces and reached towards her own weapon, the Protectress slashed at the arrow. The razor sharp blade hit in at an angle and cut it in two.

"There!" Charole spat out, hoping that she was sounding more triumphant than she felt as she held out the segment which remained in her hand.

"But what kind of tree did this come from?" Dryaka insisted, taking and staring at the hollow tube of fiber glass with an understandable lack of comprehension. "*I've* never seen wood like it."

"Or me," Charole conceded, having sheathed her sword and retrieved the other piece of the arrow. Examining the razorhead as the High Priest had done, she went on, "Nor have I seen an arrow's head to equal this one for sharpness."

If Dryaka felt any satisfaction at hearing the Protectress's admission, he gave no sign of it. In fact, he hardly seemed to be aware that she had spoken. His eyes went from the portion of the arrow in his hand, via the section she was holding, to Tomlu's body. When he looked up, there was more than a suggestion of worry on his face. Charole experienced no pleasure at this evidence of his perturbation, although under different conditions she would have. She knew what was disturbing him and she shared his concern.

Dryaka was a ruthless and ambitious man. Born in a *grar-gatah* riding family, he had clawed his way upwards until attaining his present status. The social distinctions of the Mun-Gatah were controlled by physical prowess, but rising was far from easy. Apart from becoming a member of the Council of Elders when a vacancy occurred, he could go no higher. While subject to the Council's control, he had plans for his own and their nation's aggrandizement beyond anything the six Elders suspected. In fact, outside of his immediate supporters only Charole knew—although he did not suspect it—that he wanted to conquer and rule all the nations with whom his people came into contact. She had learned by seducing, then murdering—making it look like an accident—one of his most loyal supporters.

In the opinion of the Council (when answering Dryaka's tentative proposal), going to war against the various fighting nations—as opposed to raiding them and dealing with their retaliatory attacks—would be too costly to be contemplated. Not to the Mun-Gatah warriors, whose metal helmets and leather breastplates gave considerable protection if not complete immunity, but to their mounts. Many of the zebras were sure to be killed in the battles, as enemies frequently shot or cut them down to make their riders fight on foot. Such loses would displease the Quagga God and He would not give His people the blessing they required to be assured of victory.

Less enamoured by the religion of his people than the members of the Council of Elders, although he realized its value as a means of controlling and dominating the population, Dryaka considered that the loss of the animals would be a small enough price if he achieved his desires. He had been confident that, with the aid of their protective clothing and superior organization, the Mun-Gatah could defeat every other nation in turn.

The meeting with Dawn had caused the High Priest to revise that conclusion.

From his first view of the girl's bow, Dryaka had sensed that its unusual design made it exceptionally powerful. That it had killed Tomlu was *very* convincing evidence of its full potential.

Until coming close enough to examine the scout's body, the High Priest had not appreciated just how unusual and powerful the tawny-haired beauty's weapon must be. Certainly the "wood" from which the arrow had been constructed was a very strange kind, but vastly superior to that used by the nations with whom he was acquainted. Nor had any of them possessed arrowheads of such high quality.

Apparently the mysterious "Suppliers," whose identity and purpose Dryaka had never been able to discover, had seen fit to equip the "Apes" with weapons that were far better than those given to any other nation. The thought gave rise to another that was even more intriguing.

What if Dawn should be one of the "Suppliers?"

Such a supposition would explain why Dryaka had never heard of her nation by its true name. It was also likely that their own arms would be far superior to those supplied to other people.

If Dryaka's theory should prove correct and he captured the girl, the secrets to which she might be a party would be of the greatest value. He felt sure that, once he had her in his power, he could make her divulge all her information.

Even if the High Priest was wrong in assuming that Dawn was one of the "Suppliers," holding her would still serve a very useful purpose. Recollecting what she had said about her people being great archers, he could see that they might be a major barrier against his plans for dominance. Apart from the Amazons, the other nations tended to regard their bows as tools for hunting rather than as weapons of war. When fighting, they relied upon swords, war-axes, clubs or spears and shields. So the long lances wielded by the mounted Mun-Gatahs generally out-ranged the arms of their enemies. That would not apply to the "Apes." If their warriors were so minded, their arrows would slaughter the Mun-Gatahs long before the lances could reach them. So having Dawn as a hostage would be of use in dealing with her "father."

"I wouldn't care to fight against her people, whoever they are," Charole remarked, cutting in on Dryaka's train of thought.

"Or me," the High Priest conceded, darting a glance at the woman to see if there might be some deeper meaning to her comment. He had never been entirely satisfied that Lagdok, to whom he had told his plans, had been killed by accident after having attended a banquet at the home of an Elder. Charole had also been a guest and the man had always been susceptible to feminine wiles. However, reading nothing in the beautiful features, he went on, "Of course, there's no reason why we should have to."

Before Charole could reply, a rider appeared on the ridge beyond the chasm. Reining his lathered *banargatah* to a halt at the edge, he yelled and waved a hand. Identifying the newcomer by his small size and scarlet tunic as one of the Council's messengers, Dryaka scowled. Letting the section of the arrow fall, he stalked to his quagga and mounted it. Moving almost as quickly, but retaining the portion of arrow which she had been examining, Charole returned to her mount and boarded it. They rode towards the chasm together and the rest of the party followed.

"What is it?" the High Priest demanded, on reaching the chasm.

"Zongaffa sent me to ask you if you would return to the camp immediately, my lord," the messenger answered.

"Why?" Charole asked.

"That he did not tell me, my lady," the small man replied.

Although the Protectress had failed to gather any information, she sensed that Dryaka was relieved by the message. So he was. When he had seen the messenger, he had wondered whether the Council of Elders had heard and taken exception to the orders he had given to the People-Taker. As yet he could not claim sufficient support to challenge the authority of the Elders and must yield to their desires.

The news the High Priest had been given was interesting. It implied that there were developments in something which he believed could be important and very useful. Ever since Zongaffa, the aged herbalist, had made an accidental discovery, Dryaka had believed that it could be put to practical and effective use. Perhaps the herbalist had discovered a means of doing so. If that had happened, Dryaka wanted to hear about it as soon as possible. There was only one problem. By returning to the camp, he would lose any chance of capturing Dawn and learning her secrets.

CHAPTER EIGHT

Are The Others Coming After You?

LOOKING at the man who had come from his place of concealment, Dawn Drummond-Clayton took stock of the situation and reacted swiftly. Although she had been taken by surprise and was startled at his appearance, she was not unduly alarmed. He was holding a spear, but the shape of its blade and its thick handle suggested that it was better suited to thrusting than throwing. What was more, as he was a good thirty yards away and she had already started to arm herself, she did not consider him to be too much of a threat.

Letting go of her shoulder-quiver, the girl scooped up the bow. Having done so, she liberated an arrow from the quiver that was attached to it. Setting the shaft on the handle-riser's arrow rest, she nocked the slot at its end to the string without taking her eyes from the man. Straightening and adopting her shooting posture, she commenced her draw.

Clearly the man knew what a bow and arrow was. He had started to move forward, but came to a halt as the four-bladed point was lined on his chest. While he did not have the clothing or appearance of one of the zebra riders, Dawn felt disinclined to take chances. So she retained her weapon at its position of readiness.

Holding the fletching at its anchor point, the girl studied the man. Six foot in height, he had brown skin, black hair cut after the fashion of Prince Valiant and pleasant features which reminded her of the Polynesians she had met during her travels. Broad shouldered and heavily muscled, he did not slim down at the waist as well as Bunduki. For all that, he did not convey an impression of being slow and cumbersome. His only garment was a loincloth of jaguarskin. At the left side of its belt hung a sheathed knife. Thrust through a loop on the right was a strange weapon like a short handled pole-axe. The small, hammer-like head was backed by a long, narrow, slightly curved spike. Dawn decided that it resembled a *czákan*.* Matching his height, the spear had a stout handle with a strong crossguard attached about two feet below a head that looked as though it had been made from the blade of a knife.

"Who are you?" the man inquired and once again the girl found that she could understand what was being said.

"My name is Dawn," she replied, allowing the bow's string to go forward under control but ready to draw it again if the need should arise. "Who are you?"

"I am one who is called At-Vee, the Hunter," the man answered, without making any attempt to move closer. "If you are one of the People-Taker's escort——."

"I'm not," Dawn assured him. "In fact, I don't know who the People-Taker is."

"Then you aren't a Mun-Gatah?" asked the man.

"I am *not!*" Dawn declared firmly, deducing from the sound of his voice that he did not care for the "Riders of the Zebras" and guessing who he meant. "But I've seen some of them.

"Where are they?" At-Vee demanded, glaring around in a hostile manner which gave added confirmation that he did not regard the Mun-Gatahs as friends.

"Beyond the woodland, on the plains," Dawn replied and hoped to gain an ally. "I had to kill one of them when they tried to capture me."

"Are the others coming after you?" the man asked.

"They may be," the girl admitted. "But, if so, they

*Czákan: a Polish horseman's war-hammer of the late 16th and early 17th Centuries.

aren't too close behind. I've neither seen nor heard anything of them."

"Did they have any prisoners with them?" At-Vee wanted to know, resting the butt of his spear on the ground.

"I didn't see any," Dawn confessed and, as an expression of disappointment came to his face, went on, "But I never went near their camp. It must have been on the other side of a river and was out of sight."

"Then they couldn't be the People-Taker and his escort," At-Vee said quietly and half to himself. "Joar-Fane won't be with them."

Even as the man was speaking, he started to walk slowly forward. A slight swaying of some bushes some thirty feet beyond him attracted Dawn's attention. Turning her gaze in that direction, she discovered an animal was emerging stealthily from its place of concealment. With a sensation of alarm, she identified it as a full grown tiger and knew that it was stalking At-Vee.

Crouching so low that its stomach was brushing against the ground, the great striped beast had its eyes fixed on At-Vee's broad back and its tail was whisking from side to side. Dawn knew that it would very soon be launching its attack. Already its muscles were bunching and the unsheathed claws of the hind feet dug into the ground so as to give added propulsive power when it charged.

Unlike many of her generation, probably because she had greater practical knowledge and experience, Dawn did not pretend to believe that predatory creatures never hunted and preyed upon human beings. She knew that, particularly in a primitive environment where they had not learned the deadly effects of firearms, the larger carnivores would kill and eat men, women or children just as willingly as they would animals.

With that in mind, the girl did not hesitate. Taking a long bound to her right, so as to have an unrestricted aim at the tiger, she brought up her bow and commenced the draw.

"Behind you!" Dawn shouted as she started to move.

With a deep, throaty roar, the tiger thrust itself into motion!

Although at first puzzled and not a little alarmed by the girl's behaviour, At-Vee quickly realized that she was looking at something to his rear. Obviously, she was giving a genuine warning. The roar which came to his ears, as he was already starting to turn, confirmed it. What he saw and heard told him that he was in deadly peril. The tiger was bounding towards him and would soon be close enough to make its final, killing, spring.

Dropping the butt of the spear to the ground as he completed his turn, At-Vee grasped the handle in both hands below the crossguard. At the same time, he slid his right foot forward and bent his left leg. He doubted whether he would have time to adopt his kneeling posture and brace himself correctly before the tiger was upon him.

A skilled hunter, At-Vee had on several occasions goaded a leopard or a jaguar into attacking him as he crouched behind his spear, thus allowing the beast to impale itself. There were, however, two major differences between those efforts and his present situation. Firstly, he had always been ready and had brought about the charge at his own convenience. Secondly, and even more important, the tiger was much larger and heavier than even the largest jaguar that he had dealt with.

Having adopted her shooting stance as soon as she came to a halt, Dawn completed her draw. Feeling the cold steel of the arrowhead touch her left forefinger, she aimed slightly ahead of the onrushing tiger so as to allow for its continued forward motion. Loosing the arrow, she saw it flashing away on a converging course as the great beast started to rise in the bound that would carry it onto its prey. After what seemed like an age, she heard the thud of the Razorhead meeting the animal's body just behind its shoulder. The four blades carved their way to cut a swathe through its vital organs, but that alone would not be sufficient to halt its leap.

Watching the tiger hurtling towards him, At-Vee expected to be killed. He had his left knee on the ground and the spear rose before him, but he was not as firmly positioned as he would have been if granted a few more seconds. His posture might have been suitable when receiving the charge of a leopard, or even a jaguar. It would not stand up against the weight of the tiger. There was, however, nothing he could do except brace himself as securely as possible and hope for a miracle.

The miracle happened!

Feeling the agony caused by the arrow driving through its flesh, even though there was not the solid impact and shock force of a bullet, the tiger gave a choking howl and its body curved in mid-flight. While it still went towards the man, its forelegs and great, hook-like claws were directed away from him. Instead of hitting the chest, the point of the spear spiked home alongside the arrow but entered at a less acute angle.

When the tiger collided with the spear, its weight threw At-Vee off balance. He felt pain sear through his right leg as the ankle buckled under him. Fortunately it was not so severe that it numbed his thought processes. Releasing the spear as soon as the tiger was impaled, he threw himself to the right. On landing, he sent his right hand to the head of the war-hammer on his belt and slid it from its retaining loop.

Reaching for another arrow, Dawn watched the great beast land on the spear and At-Vee fling himself from underneath it. The tip of the blade was just emerging from the striped flank when the crossguard prevented it from going any further. Crashing to the ground, the stricken tiger roared and thrashed wildly in an agonized frenzy. Then it went limp.

"Are you hurt?" Dawn inquired, turning her eyes

from the tiger and looking to where the man was trying to rise.

"It's my leg," At-Vee replied, sinking back to sit on the ground. "I think it's broken!"

"Let me look at it," Dawn offered, walking forward.

"Why would you want to help me?" At-Vee challenged, a wary glint coming into his eyes as he tightened his grip on the war-hammer's handle.

"I helped you against the tiger," Dawn reminded him. "And I believe that the Mun-Gatah are enemies of both of us."

Turning his gaze to the great striped shape, At-Vee noticed for the first time that the fletching of an arrow thrust out of it close to his spear. Then, apart from one detail, everything became clear to him. He realized why the tiger had behaved so oddly while springing at him. If the girl had not used her bow with such deadly effect, it would have come down upon the spear with its forelegs thrust ahead and claws positioned so that they could have found his flesh.

The only puzzling point was why his rescuer had loosed her arrow. There would have been little or no danger of the tiger turning on her if she had fled, as it would have been fully occupied with him. So he wondered why she had helped him. Nothing in the few contacts he had had with members of other nations had led him to expect friendship or help at a foreigner's hands.

"I'll put down my bow and let you hold my knife," Dawn went on with a smile, "if that will prove I'm a friend."

"There's no need for that," At-Vee stated, and placed his war-hammer on the ground, sensing that he could trust her. He also realized that, if his leg should be broken, retaining her assistance would be all that stood between him and almost certain death. "Thank you for offering to help."

Before starting to examine the man's leg, Dawn collected her shoulder-quiver. She laid it and her bow alongside his weapons and knelt down. Placing her left hand under his right calf, she raised and studied his swollen ankle. Taking hold of his foot with the other hand, she moved it gently. Although perspiration beaded his face and he half closed his eyes in pain, he made no sound.

"It's not broken," Dawn announced, lowering the limb gently to the ground. "But it is badly sprained and you won't be able to use it for some time."

"I have to do and find Joar-Fane!" At-Vee gritted, sitting up.

"Who is that?" Dawn asked, looking around for the means to render further aid.

"She was to be my wife. I had brought back a jaguar's skin for her father to make my claim," At-Vee explained, trying to rise. "But when I arrived, I found that the Mun-Gatahs' People-Taker had taken her."

"You stay where you are!" Dawn commanded, laying a hand on his shoulder. "If you try to walk, you'll only make your ankle worse."

"But Joar-Fane—!" At-Vee began, sinking back.

"She won't be any better off if you cripple yourself and can't walk at all," Dawn pointed out. "Where is the nearest water?"

"I passed a stream not far away."

"Do you think that you can walk there with my help?"

"I can."

"That's good," Dawn said. "When we get there, I'll see what I can do about your ankle."

"Can you get my spear for me?" At-Vee requested.

"I'll try," the girl promised and glanced at the empty place on her bow-quiver. "And I'll see if I can pull my arrow out while I'm doing it."

Going to the tiger, Dawn examined it. Her arrow had buried itself in the body almost to the fletching which would make removal difficult. If she gripped the part that showed, she would crush the feathers of the fletching and ruin them. Yet she had no desire to lose another arrow. There were not a commodity which she could replenish in the primitive jungle. Certainly there would be no way in which she could obtain any fiber glass Micro-Flites, particularly if her theory regarding her whereabouts should prove true.

Putting the arrow from her mind for the moment, Dawn took hold of the spear's hand with both hands. Placing her right foot on the carcass, she began to pull with all her far from inconsiderable strength. Conscious of At-Vee studying her and sensing the admiration he was feeling towards her, she continued to exert her full muscular power. At first the weapon held firm. Then, slowly, an inch at a time, it began to move. With a final heave, she drew it out.

With the spear removed, Dawn laid it aside and drew her knife. Knowing what she must do next, she made a wry face and set to work cutting the arrow free. Even with the razor edge of the Randall Model 1 fighting knife's eight-inch long, clip-pointed blade, it was a lengthy and messy task. She was not sorry when she had accomplished it.

Wiping her hands, the knife's blade, the arrow and the spear as clean as she could on the grass, Dawn turned her attention to At-Vee. He was sitting with her bow in his hands and studying it with rapt attention.

"I've never seen the like of this before," the man declared, in tones of awe, laying the bow down as she returned. "Do all your people have such weapons?"

"Yes," Dawn replied, which was true as far as it went. Being keen archers, every member of her family owned a modern hunting bow of similar quality. Handing him his spear, she knelt and attached the arrow to the bow-quiver. "I'll help you to the stream if you're ready."

Giving his assent to the suggestion, At-Vee allowed the girl to help him rise. He placed his left arm across her shoulders and used the spear with the right for extra support.

"Who are your people?" At-Vee inquired, being genuinely interested and also wanting to take his mind from the pain that walking, even with assistance, was causing.

"You wouldn't know them," Dawn answered. "Our chief is Tarzan of the Apes."

"I have never heard of him, or of your people," At-Vee stated, which was what the girl had expected although hoping that she would receive the opposite information. "Are all the 'Apes' great hunters?"

Remembering the gold-clad woman's use of the name "Apes," the significance of the way her companion's question had been worded struck Dawn. It implied that, no matter what language they were employing, she had given Tarzan's name in English.

"Yes," Dawn confirmed truthfully, putting the phenomenon aside to be considered and discussed when she was reuinited with Bunduki.

"Are your people near by?" At-Vee asked.

"My—husband—Bunduki isn't too far way," Dawn answered. While she believed that she could trust the man, she also felt it was advisable to let him think she was married and her 'husband' was in the vicinity. "He is one of the greatest hunters and fighters of the 'Apes'."

Much as At-Vee would have liked to satisfy his curiosity regarding the girl's weapons, he refrained. All of them, including the knife (if the ease with which it had cut out the arrow was anything to go by), were far superior to anything he had ever seen. The point was verified when, changing the subject, he inquired about her escape from the Mun-Gatahs and learned she had killed one by sending an arrow through his leather breastplate. According to the Telonga legends, such a garment was so strong that its wearer could not be harmed. However, among his people, the matter of the mysterious "Suppliers" was tabu except to the Elders of each village and must not be discussed by anybody else.

On reaching the banks of the small stream, Dawn helped At-Vee to seat himself and, while he was dangling the injured foot in the water, sought for a means of treating it. Finding a plant with broad leaves, of a kind which she had never seen before, she gathered some of them. Then she collected some of a moss-like growth and thin reeds, using them all to make a cold compress which she applied to his ankle.

With his ankel bandaged by the plants, At-Vee accepted Dawn's offer of a meal. He was puzzled by the *pemmican* and *biltong* that she produced from her quiver, but after tasting them admitted they were good. Then he told her what had brought him to that part of the woodland.

On learning that the Mun-Gatahs' People-Taker had claimed his intended wife, Joar-Fane, in his absence, At-Vee had set off to try to rescue her. However, he had found tracks which suggested that she had escaped from her captors and fled into the jungle pursued by some of them. Following, he had crossed what he called the Big River which served as a boundary between the Telongas' country and that of the "Hairy People." The previous evening he had lost the tracks due to a herd of elephants passing over and obliterating them. Knowing that the Mun-Gatahs lived somewhere on the plains, he had been heading in that direction hoping to pick up the trail again.

There were a number of questions which Dawn would have liked to have put to At-Vee, but the opportunity did not arise. Faint noises came to their ears, causing them to stare in the direction from which they had come. The girl's eyes turned to meet the man's. Although the sounds were still a good distance away, both knew that they were hearing hooves and human voices.

"It must be the Mun-Gatahs!" Dawn breathed. "They're following my tracks."

"How many of them are there?" At-Vee asked, glancing at his injured ankle.

"At least nine, if they've all crossed the river," Dawn answered, speaking no louder than the man. "There may be even more for all I know."

"We can't fight them, even if there are only nine," At-Vee declared bitterly. "And with my ankle like this, I can't run fast enough to escape. But you must go. They'll show you no mercy now you've killed one of them."

Dawn did not reply for several seconds, but she was thinking fast. As At-Vee had pointed out, they could not hope to beat off a determined attack by the Mun-Gatahs and she still retained sufficient of her civilized upbringing to want to avoid further killing if it was possible. Although she felt sure that she could escape from her mounted pursuers, given that much of a start and in wooded country, flight was out of the question for her companion.

There was, the girl realized, only one answer.

"Take my bow and arrows, At-Vee!" Dawn said urgently. "Then go and hide in the bushes."

"What are you doing to do?" the man asked.

"Draw them away from you," Dawn replied.

"But——!" At-Vee began.

"It's our only chance," the girl declared, and smiled confidently. "They might be riding, but I can travel faster than them through this type of country. Particularly as I won't be hampered with my bow."

Without waiting for any further debate on the matter, Dawn darted off towards the sounds of the riders. She wanted to come into contact with them before they found the tiger's body and discovered that she had a companion. If they were following her trail, whoever was doing the tracking would be able to deduce that At-Vee was injured from the signs he and she had left and might guess what she was trying to do.

Clearly the Mun-Gatahs were not travelling at any speed. That was only to be expected. Although Dawn had not made any determined effort to hide the signs of her passage, following the marks left by her bare feet would not be easy. Travelling at a fast walk, wanting to conserve her strength and energy for the flight that would come when they saw her, she had gone about fifty yards beyond the tiger when she received her first sight of them.

Halting behind a tree, Dawn studied the composition of the party. Neither of the quagga riders were present, but that still left two women and five men to contend with. The eagle's attendant was in the lead, walking and studying the ground, with his zebra following on his heels like a well-trained dog. All his companions were mounted and, although the girl could not hear what was being said, the women appeared to be talking in low but heated tones. She wondered whether she was the topic of their conversation and concluded that it was likely.

There was no time for Dawn to dwell on such futile speculation. Although the Mun-Gatahs were still about a hundred yards away, the terrain through which they were passing would still favour them. She had known it when making her suggestion to At-Vee but was willing to take a chance if it would prevent them from finding the helpless hunter.

Drawing in a breath, Dawn walked from behind the tree as if she did not know her pursuers were so close. Hearing a shout, which informed her that she had been seen, she threw a look at them. Then, as she turned and started to run, she wished that Bunduki was in the vicinity. She also hoped that, wherever he was, he was not in any kind of danger. Hearing the commotion behind her, she put all such thoughts from her head.

The chase was on and she would need all her wits about her if she was to avoid being captured, or killed!

CHAPTER NINE

She Isn't As Good A Lover As Me

AT about the time that Dawn was starting to run away from the Mun-Gatahs, Bunduki and Joar-Fane were finishing their meal.

While the blond giant could have made a fire easily enough, even though he had no matches, he had not wished to do so. The rising smoke would have been a sure indication to any hostile force such as the Mun-Gatahs' People-Takers—whoever, or whatever, they might be—or other human beings in the vicinity. When he had explained this to the girl, he had discovered that it would not be necessary. Delighted at being able to talk after the silence which he had insisted upon as they were walking, she had said that her people frequently ate raw meat. So had he, on expeditions when his adoptive family had reverted to living in a primitive fashion.

"Never have I seen such a beautiful man as you, Bunduki," Joar-Fane purred after they had eaten and washed their hands and face in the stream. She smiled at him in a way that had never failed to win over any man she was trying to attract.

"That's what Dawn tells me," the blond giant replied.

"Do you already have a wife?" Joar-Fane asked, sounding disappointed but not unduly perturbed. "Or have you many?"

"I've never needed more than one," Bunduki stated, hoping to kill off any notions that the girl was harbouring.

"She isn't as good a lover as me," Joar-Fane declared. "I can make love better than any other Telonga maiden. Shall I show you, Bunduki?"

"Not right now," the big blond growled hastily, for her hands were hooking under the monkey-skin halter.

"At-Vee has told me many times how well I can make love," Joar-Fane protested.

"Who is that?" Bunduki inquired.

"A hunter," the girl replied, pouting but refraining from removing the garment. "The best in our village—but he is not as great as you."

"Is he your husband?"

"No!"

"Does he want to be?"

"Of course," Joar-Fane confirmed, sounding as if that was a foregone conclusion. "He has brought much meat to my father's house and many skins. We have made love many times."

"Have you had children?" Bunduki asked.

"No!" the girl yelped, displaying shock at such a suggestion. "That would not be proper until we are married. How many children have you and Dawn?"

"None yet," the blond giant admitted, hiding his amusement at her indignation. He decided that, in view of her reply, a change of subject might be advisable. "Did the People-Taker claim At-Vee too?"

"No. He was away from the village, or the Elders would have put him away with the rest of the hunters," Joar-Fane answered, moving closer and reaching to take hold of Bunduki's hands in her own. "Must we talk about such things?"

"Dawn is very good at talking and always explains the things I want to know," the big blond said craftily, freeing himself and sitting down. "That is one of the reasons why I love her."

"I'm very good at explaining things," Joar-Fane declared, looking at him in a calculating manner and doing as he had hoped she would. Sitting by his side, she went on, "What do you want to know?"

Guided by Bunduki's questions and determined to

prove that she was superior to Dawn—who she assumed was his wife—the girl started to tell him about her own people.

The Telonga were in general a pleasure-seeking nation much given to such peaceful pursuits as singing, dancing and making love. In all of these, particularly the last, Joar-Fane claimed to have no equal.

When her hint failed to elicit the response she was hoping for, the girl continued with her description. Her people lived in several large villages scattered through an area of jungle bounded by the "Land With No Trees," two wide rivers and what, from her account, was either a large lake or an ocean, possibly the latter, as she said men who had been there claimed the water tasted salty.

With the majority of their needs in life supplied by a bounteous nature, most of the Telongas were content to follow a leisurely existence not overburdened by hard work. There were, however, a few hunters in every community. Restless, active men, they were regarded with suspicion by the rest of the population despite having such uses as suppliers of meat and skins, or defenders against any wild beasts which plagued the villages. Joar-Fane declared that, as they were excellent lovers when so inclined, on the whole she approved of them.

From what she said when Bunduki brought the matter up, there was no kind of organized fighting force for the protection of their homes and territory.

"We don't need such a thing," Joar-Fane insisted. "We don't have any enemies."

"How about the Mun-Gatahs' People-Taker?" Bunduki challenged.

Apparently the Telonga villagers, with a few exceptions, took the periodic visits by the People-Taker and his escort for granted, regarding them as a small price to pay for an otherwise untroubled existence. They came, selected several—but never too many—maidens and young men, departing without disruption of the remainder's pleasures.

Only the hunters were inclined to resist the levy, but they were invariably "put away" by the Elders before the People-Taker arrived. Joar-Fane neither knew nor cared how the "putting away" was accomplished. The hunters were always returned alive, unharmed, and in good loving condition, which was good enough for her even if the subject had not been tabu as a matter for discussion.

Nor did the girl have any idea why the People-Taker collected the young men and women. It was obvious to Bunduki, from what she said, that she had hoped the selected maidens were destined to become the wives of handsome and lusty Mun-Gatah men; but she had been disillusioned on that point. At first, having had a quarrel with At-Vee because he had insisted on leaving the village instead of remaining and attending a dance that was being given by one of her friends, she had been delighted at being among those selected. However, once away from the village, she had found that the male members of the People-Taker's escort were not interested in making love and her attempts at stimulating such a desire had been thwarted in a painful manner by one of the Mun-Gatah women.

What was more, the Mun-Gatahs had proved to be harsh and cruel. Remarks which Joar-Fane had overheard had warned her that she might not be going to the pleasant life which she had anticipated. So, showing more courage and initiative than Bunduki would have imagined her to possess, she had escaped after they had made camp for the night. Unfortunately for her, she had got hopelessly lost. Then, with the party sent after her by the People-Taker on her trail, she had been driven even deeper into the jungle. She had fallen into the Big River and, although she could swim well enough to have been in no danger of drowning, the strength of the current had carried her across.

Knowing that she was in the land of the "Hairy People," about whom the hunters had told so many frightening stories, the girl had been forced to leave the river because of the persistence of her pursuers. Although she had not seen any sign of them that day, she had kept moving in the hope of returning to the river and swimming over, then finding her way home. Instead, she had been located by *Bul-Mok* and his family. Fleeing from them, Bunduki had saved her.

While eager to please the blond giant by explaining about the People-Taker, Joar-Fane forgot to mention two points of interest. She had said that the Mun-Gatahs made visits twice a year, following the ends of the two rainy seasons. In her eagerness to start the business of love-making, she overlooked the fact that the latest collection had been made in the dry season and also that it had consisted of more maidens and young men than was usual.

"What do you know about the Mun-Gatahs?" Bunduki asked, as the girl lay on her back in an attitude which implied that she had talked enough and felt it was time for her reward.

Annoyance flickered across Joar-Fane's face and she sat up. Then she smiled in a knowing manner. At-Vee had been a much more satisfactory love maker than the blond giant was proving. However, he too had also been slow at getting down to the serious business of wooing. When he finally did, the results had always been worth waiting for. That would, she felt sure, apply just as much in Bunduki's case. Being shrewd in such matters, she decided that she would have to humour him until he was ready to commence.

Sitting at the side of the small girl, Bunduki had to admit that she was superbly proportioned and voluptuous. As a healthy young man in the peak of physical condition, he could not help being attracted by her. However, he was determined to hold himself in check. Joar-Fane's race and colour had nothing to do with the decision. None of his adoptive kinsmen had been promiscuous. In fact, they had all been notable for their unswerving loyalty and devotion to their respective wives. Nor had Bunduki ever become embroiled in the so-called New Morality which had infested the western world. Even during the short period he had spent in

England, he had avoided becoming entangled in its meshes. Having always had to be self-reliant instead of dependent upon the British Welfare State, he did not need to use sexual prowess to conceal a lack of other masculine achievements. What was more, at that moment, he had other things of greater importance on his mind.

Suddenly, Bunduki found his thoughts turning to Dawn; but not in the way that they had done constantly since waking in the tree. Up to that moment he had always regarded her almost as a younger sister; a delightful playmate and a tomboy who was willing to try anything that he was attempting. While aware that she had grown into a very beautiful, shapely and attractive young woman, his opinions along that line had previously been those a brother might have felt. Looking at Joar-Fane, he started to think of his adoptive cousin for the first time as a most desirable member of the opposite sex.

The little Telonga girl would have been furious if she had guessed the kind of thoughts which she had brought about. Being unaware of them, she did her best to stimulate her rescuer's interest and desire to make love.

There was little enough that Jor-Fane could tell Bunduki about the Mun-Gatah people. According to what she had heard, the men were big, muscular and very fierce. Although the People-Taker and his escort had never arrived at her village clad in such garments, the hunters claimed they wore metal helmets and breast-plates of leather that no weapon could pierce. They were armed with what she described as long knives and spears. Although the women she had seen were not exactly ugly—she refused to admit that they had been beautiful and curvaceous—they did not appear to be interested in making love. She regarded that as being most peculiar. More so, in fact, than that the party invariably arrived riding on strange hornless animals with black and white striped skins. At-Vee had said that all the Mun-Gatah people had such animals and many more roamed wild in the "Land With No Trees," but they were never seen in the jungle except when brought by the People-Taker's party.

Bunduki found the girl's information, scanty as it was, more baffling than helpful. In fact, nothing he had heard made sense. The strange, hornless black and white animals sounded like zebras, which implied he was somewhere near the plains of Africa as did the description, the "Land With No Trees." Except that no wild zebra had a suitable physical confirmation of riding or draught work. Nor was there any sizeable area of the African plains that had not been explored, or at least flown over. A tribe, or a nation, who rode zebras would surely have been discovered.

If it came to the point, there was little or no undiscovered land of any kind left in the world; certainly not one of sufficient size that could offer jungles, plains, big rivers and such a diversity of human and animal life. Counting the *Mangani* the blond giant had already heard of three nations.

"Are there any other people?" Bunduki asked when the girl once more stopped speaking and looked at him hopefully. "I mean apart from the Telonga, Mun-Gatah and the 'Hairy Men'?"

"The old men tell us about somebody they called the Gruziak who used to come to our villages," Joar-Fane sighed, wishing that the blond giant would stop asking such uninteresting questions and make love instead. "They were warriors with red skins and rode animals like the Mun-Gatahs', except they weren't striped and were of different colours. I've never seen them. The Mun-Gatahs drove them away. And I have heard it said that there is another nation of nothing but women. They don't have any men at all. But I don't believe there is anybody like that."

"You wouldn't," Bunduki thought and smiled.

"Do you want to tell me about your people?" Joar-Fane inquired, having seen the smile and hoping it heralded what she had been waiting for. "Where are they?"

"That's what I'd like to know," the blond giant said to himself.

The reference to the red-skinned Gruziaks, with their mounts that looked like the Mun-Gatahs' zebras —if that was the identity of the creatures—but variously coloured and not striped, suggested a nation of horsemen. Perhaps the girl was making them and the female warriors—who apart from their men-less state were suggestive of the Grecian Amazons*—up out of her imagination in order to impress him and bring him to a suitable frame of mind for her purposes.

When Bunduki did not reply to her question, Joar-Fane felt that success and fulfilment were within her grasp. She was certain that the time had come for something far more interesting and diverting than chattering about other people. Smiling, she reached across and laid a hot little hand on Bunduki's left bicep.

Even as the blond giant was seeking a way to refuse which would not offend the girl, one was presented to him. From far away to the north-west came an eerie, high-pitched and almost wailing cry.

Instantly, Bunduki sprang to his feet. Ignoring Joar-Fane's squeak of mingled annoyance, protest and frustration, he stared in the direction from which the sound had originated. Faint though it had been, he knew it was the distress call of a female *Mangani*.

However, the call was from such a long distance that the blond giant could not make a positive identification. Nor was it repeated, so he was unable to gain further information.

Bunduki found himself faced with a difficult decision. While the distress call had come from the direction in which his instincts suggested that Dawn could be found, there were *Mangani* in the jungle. Any reply he made would be heard by the family who claimed the

*According to the legends, the Grecian Amazons maintained their race by having intercourse with men from neighbouring districts. After which, any male children were either killed or returned to their fathers.

territory and would almost certainly be investigated if they were close enough.

There was more to the problem than the danger from the territorial bull. The call had originated from so far away that, even if he did not have Joar-Fane with him, the blond giant knew he could not get there in time to deal with whatever was threatening his adoptive cousin, should she be the one who had made it.

CHAPTER TEN

Don't Kill Her, Damn You!

"I don't like it," Sabart stated, glancing around her in a worried manner. "The foreign bitch is going into the land of the 'Hairy People'."

"You can always turn back," Elidor spat out. While equally perturbed, her rival's words had the effect of making her determined to keep going. A malicious smile flickered on her face as she continued, "I don't intend to. And, anyway, there shouldn't be any danger. Charole told us the foreign bitch wouldn't dare enter the jungle."

When Dryaka had ordered his faction to follow Dawn, the Protectress had said that her adherents would accompany them. As the High Priest had known that the eagle's attendant was a very capable tracker and might be useful in following Dawn, and as he was not enamoured with the idea of riding to the main camp in the company of Charole's supporters, even with the Council of Elders' messenger present, he had agreed.

Discussing how the foreign girl might act, Charole had proved to share Dryaka's theory that she would, in all probability, avoid penetrating too deeply into the woodland. Unfortunately, the Mun-Gatahs' party found that she was doing so, and was showing no sign of turning towards the plains. Instead, she seemed to be determined to enter the jungle, even though it was the domain of the "Hairy People."

Already the terrain was becoming difficult for the Mun-Gatahs to traverse it in a compact group. If the

117

trees and bushes should grow in closer proximity, they would be compelled to ride in single file. Doing so would render them even more vulnerable to ambush and attack, especially if the girl belonged to a warrior race which made its home in such country. None of them had any desire to fight against archers as skilled as she had been, particularly when they were armed with bows of the kind that had killed Tomlu. However, as neither faction would allow their rivals to see they were worried, each waited and hoped the other would suggest that they went back.

"Look!" snapped one of Dryaka's male adherents, pointing ahead. "It's her!"

Following the direction indicated by the speaker, the rest of the party saw Dawn. They were relieved to notice that she was no longer carrying the bow and quiver of arrows, although there was no time for them to consider and discuss the omission. Becoming aware of their presence, she turned and started to run away.

"Get after her!" Sabart screamed.

Despite the rest of the party's eagerness to follow the order, there was some confusion for a few seconds. To allow the eagle's attendant an unrestricted view of the girl's tracks, the rest of the party had been compelled to let him take the lead and walk ahead of them. On seeing the killer of his bird, belatedly, as his eyes had been on her trail rather than watching his surroundings, he let out a shriek of rage that was reminiscent of the cry the eagle had given as it was plunging towards its intended victim. Turning, he leapt towards his well-trained zebra. Obediently, knowing what was expected of it, the *grar-gatah* swung at an angle which would allow him to reach the saddle. Vaulting astride, without touching the stirrups, he snatched the reins from the saddlehorn. In mounting as he had, he was blocking his companions' paths and preventing them from giving chase.

"Get out of the way, you stupid *grar-gatah!*" Elidor screeched, having sent her mount bounding forward in an attempt to get ahead of the other woman.

Ignoring the angry yell, particularly because it had emanated from a member of the rival faction, the attendant set his zebra into motion. Behind him, the angry *banar-gatah* riders combined in heaping invective on his head as they followed. Hot for revenge, he took no more notice than he had of Elidor's comment. Instead, he urged his *grar-gatah* to a reckless gallop.

Although the two women and four men sat animals which were superior to the attendant's mount, the nature of their surroundings was against them in their efforts to overtake him. Skilled riders as they all were, none was willing to exhibit the complete disregard for danger displayed by the small man as he guided his fast-moving *grar-gatah* through the trees.

Elidor and Sabart began to draw ahead of the male *banar-gatah* riders. Not only were they lighter, but their armament also gave them an advantage. Each had a short throwing spear, which Dawn had not been able to see from her side of the chasm. It was carried in two loops that were attached to the bottom of the saddle's left side skirt so as to leave the owner's hands free. The men's nine foot lances could not be carried in such a fashion. Ideal as they were for hunting or fighting on the plains, the lances were poorly adapted for use in even comparatively open woodland.

Running swiftly through the trees, Dawn could hear the hooves of her pursuers' mounts and sensed that one was approaching much faster than the rest. She fought down the temptation to look behind, knowing that she must devote all her attention to watching where she was going. At that moment, she was in two minds over the wisdom of having left her bow and arrows with the injured Telonga hunter. Without them, she could move at a faster pace and more easily. However, she did not have them to use if she needed to defend herself.

About fifty yards ahead, there was an extensive area of fairly dense bushes. Dawn made for it, growing more and more aware that one of her pursuers was rapidly closing with her. For all that, she resisted the temptation to increase her pace. If she did so prematurely, she would run herself into such a state of exhaustion that she would collapse. Instead, she scanned the wall of foliage. It would offer her concealment and could not be ridden through.

First, however, Dawn had to find a way to enter the bushes!

Having done so, she had to reach it before the first of the riders caught up with her!

Not far to her right, Dawn detected the entrance to a game trail. It was fairly wide, probably having been made by rhinoceros, elephants, or buffalo for she had seen evidence that all three species occupied the woodland. If she was to make use of the track, her pursuers would be able to ride along it.

Searching for an alternative, the girl saw that there was a smaller path on her left. Unfortunately, it was at a greater distance than the one at her right.

Would Dawn have sufficient time to reach the more suitable entrance?

The hooves were getting *very* close now!

"Don't kill her, damn you!" screamed an irate feminine voice from beyond the girl's nearest pursuer.

Hearing the words, Dawn chanced a quick glance over her shoulder. She had expected the leading rider to be fairly near, but not in such close proximity. It was, as she had guessed, the eagle's attendant. Rage and hatred distorted his face as he bore down on her as swiftly as his hard-driven zebra could travel. His right hand was grasping a sword ready for use.

Dawn doubted, from his expression, whether the man would heed the woman's shouted instructions. So she started to think how she might avoid being cut down.

Having seen the attendant draw his sword and being aware of how bitterly he had resented the death of his eagle, Elidor had screamed out her warning. When it did not appear to have any effect, she turned her head to glare at the smaller but equally voluptuous woman who was riding stirrup to stirrup with her.

"If that damned *grar-gatah* kills her, I'll see him sent to the Quagga God!" the brunette warned her rival. "Dryaka wants her alive!"

"So does Charole," Sabart answered and looked back at the male *banar-gatah* riders. "Chanak! Make him stop!"

With the man who had been addressed bawling a warning, the two women swerved to pass on either side of a tree's trunk. They did not attempt to resume the conversation when they came in sight of each other again. Instead, they watched as the attendant drew closer to the fleeing girl. From what they could see, he had no intention of taking advice or orders and had forgotten that both the High Priest and the Protectress wanted her captured alive and uninjured if possible.

Measuring the rapidly diminishing distance between himself and the girl, the attendant rose on his stirrups so that he could get added force behind a blow. In his fury at seeing her, he had completely forgotten that his party were supposed to take her prisoner and was preparing to cut her down with his sword.

Waiting until the head of his zebra was almost level with her left shoulder, thus approaching the ideal position from which to deliver a slash at her, for she believed he might choose to ignore the commands that had been yelled at him—Dawn suddenly changed direction. Implementing the scheme which she had thought out, she swerved in front of the animal. In passing, she whipped her left hand around to slap the near side of the zebra's muzzle and let out the most hideous shriek she could manage after having run so far and fast.

The unexpected blow and the yell startled the little *grar-gatah* and caused it to shy. Tossing its head wildly, it threw up its front legs and went into a rearing turn. Tensed ready to deliver a blow that would have cleft open his victim's skull, the attendant watched her disappear ahead of his mount. A moment later he was almost toppled backwards by its erratic behaviour. Only by dropping his sword and grabbing the horn in

both hands, while his legs clamped tightly against the
saddle's skirts, did he prevent himself from falling
onto the rack that had been used as a perch for the
eagle. Recovering his equilibrium with an effort that
demanded every bit of his riding skill, he found that he
was being carried away from the girl. Muttering invective, he reined the *grar-gatah* around in a hurried and
brutal fashion. By the time he was once more facing
her, she was far beyond his reach.

Satisfied that she had averted the danger of being
struck down by the man's sword, Dawn lengthened her
stride. With the sheath of the Randall knife slapping
against her bare thigh, she built up her speed as if she
had been sprinting for the finishing line in a foot-race.
Conscious of her pursuers' angry shouts, she reached
the bushes. The mouth of the second game trail, towards which her evasion had allowed her to head, was
barely wide enough for her to enter. With the foliage
brushing her arms on either side, she knew that the
Mun-Gatahs would not be able to ride in after her. On
foot, she was sure that she could hold her own.

As Dawn had expected, the bushes were higher than
the top of her yead and the trail wound in such a fashion that she was soon hidden from the entrance. Moving on at a slower pace, she replenished her lungs and
wiped the perspiration from her brow. She did not
allow herself to grow over confident and she remained
alert for any evidence that the pursuit was being continued.

Leaning over, without slackening his *grar-gatah's*
pace, the attendant scooped up his sword from where it
had fallen, its point stuck in the ground. Then he made
for the opening into which the girl had disappeared.
The rest of his party were rapidly approaching but he
ignored them. Seeing that there was no way of riding
after her, he sprang from his saddle. He felt uneasy, for
the girl had already passed out of sight and he had the
Mun-Gatahs' inborn distrust of thickly overgrown terrain. However, hatred overrode his other emotions and
he plunged forward.

"Warn him not to kill her, Sabart!" Elidor ordered, being determined to fix the blame on the other woman if the attendant repeated his attempted disobedience of their leaders' wishes.

"Take her alive, Shanu!" Sabart shouted, knowing what had prompted the brunette's words. "If you kill her, I'll have you and all your family given to the Quagga God!"

For all the notice he took, the attendant might have been stone deaf. Without so much as a glance at his companions as they dashed up, he went along the track beyond their range of vision.

Bringing their *banar-gatahs* to a halt at the edge of the bushes, the two women gazed at the mouth of the track. They did not offer to dismount, but waited for their four male companions to join them.

"Can you see anything of the girl, Elidor?" asked the senior of the High Priest's adherents, standing on his stirrups as he tried to peer over the bushes.

"No, Mador," the brunette answered. "Charole's man has gone in after her. If he catches her, he'll kill her. Lord Dryaka doesn't want her dead."

"*I've* tried shouting to him, but he's so angry he won't listen," Sabart protested petulantly and looked in a pointed fashion at the rival faction. "Somebody should go in and make him do as he's told."

"He's *Charole's* man," Mador pointed out, the words having been aimed chiefly at him. "So if he kills her——."

"He's not likely to catch her in there, she's used to that kind of country," Chanak answered, as leader of the Protectress's faction. Like the other man, he did not relish the thought of entering the narrow trail. "We'd better go around and be waiting for her when she comes out."

"The bushes look as if they go for a fair way in each direction," Mador objected. "Even if she goes straight through, she'll probably have left before we get to the other side."

"She's not likely to stay in there, Shanu will drive

her out even if he doesn't catch her," Chanak countered. "I'm going around."

"We'll leave a man each to watch this side, then the rest of us can split up and go around," Mador suggested. "Come on. She'll get away for sure if we sit talking."

With that, the High Priest's male and female adherents turned to the right. Leaving their companion, Elidor and Mador rode off at a trot.

"Stay here, Stafak!" Chanak ordered, swinging his *banar-gatah* to the left.

"I hope that fool doesn't kill her," Sabart remarked, nodding towards the bushes as she and Chanak went along the edge. "But he will if he catches her. If *that* happens, none of them must get back alive to tell Dryaka about it."

Walking swiftly along the trail, which was widening slightly, Dawn wondered what to do for the best. Clearly the Mun-Gatahs were determined to capture her. So they would come in after her, or try to prevent her from leaving until she was driven out by hunger and thirst. Most probably they would adopt the former alternative. The latter would take far too long and was likely to offer her too many opportunities to escape.

Even as she came to that conclusion, the girl heard certain significant sounds on the path behind her. Her bare feet made no noise, so she had little difficulty in detecting those made by a pursuer's sandals.

One, or more?

Turning around, Dawn could not see whoever was following her. However, she decided it was only one man. Probably the eagle's attendant. The expression of hatred on his face when he was trying to kill her from the back of his zebra suggested that he would not have given up because the attempt had failed.

Swinging around and walking on, Dawn placed her right hand on the Sambar staghorn "finger-grip" handle of her Randall knife. For a moment, she toyed with the idea of taking cover and springing on the man as he went by. Then her civilized instincts revolted against such an act. Instead, she thought there might be another course of action that would serve her purpose.

While talking as they had walked to the stream, At-Vee had expressed much concern over Joar-Fane being alone in the land of the "Hairy People." From his description, which she suspected might have been somewhat highly-coloured regarding their blood-thirsty habits and ferocity, she believed that he was referring to the *Mangani*. He had claimed that all of his people feared them. That might apply even more to a nation of plains' dwellers like the Mun-Gatah, provided they knew of the "Hairy People" and were aware that they were very close to that mysterious race's domain.

Deciding that she had nothing to lose by putting her idea to the test, for the man's footsteps warned he was coming nearer, Dawn halted and tossed back her head. From her lips burst the distress cry of a she-*Mangani*. While the female's call lacked the deep and awesome menace of a bull's challenge or victory roars, it was still an ear-tingling and eerie sound.

Almost before the last note of Dawn's call died away, nearly drowning the startled exclamation which came from very close behind her, she heard an explosive "whoof" not far in front of her.

It was the sound made by a black rhinoceros that had been disturbed!

There was a crackling of broken foliage and the bushes ahead of Dawn were agitated violently as the huge beast lurched to its feet.

As its kind always did when surprised, disturbed or alarmed, the rhinoceros rushed forward. Pure chance directed it towards the girl. She knew that it was not making a deliberate charge, but merely trying to escape and avoid contact with whatever creature had caused the unexpected noise. For all that, its actions were just as dangerous as if it was meaning to attack her.

Despite the trail having widened slightly, Dawn knew that there was not sufficient room for her to spring aside at the last moment and allow the beast to blunder by. Nor would turning and running away by of any greater use. Even if the Mun-Gatah had not been blocking her retreat, the rhinoceros was capable of much greater speed than she could attain.

CHAPTER ELEVEN

They've Caught The Foreign Bitch!

DISCARDING the idea of flight, Dawn took the only action which was left to her. Darting forward as if to meet the onrushing black rhinoceros, she watched until its head dropped ready to hook up at her. Timing the move perfectly, she leapt high into the air. Spreading her legs apart, she passed over the long anterior horn as it jerked upwards. Her hands slapped on to the huge beast's back and helped to thrust her onwards almost as if she was playing leapfrog. Aided by her own and the animal's forward momentum, she was propelled over its rump to land on the ground.

There was a startled yell from somewhere to the girl's rear as she ran forward the few steps needed to let her regain her equilibrium. Another furious snort burst from the rhinoceros, followed by a piercing and agony-filled human scream. Having recovered control of her movements, she came to a halt and spun around. She found that the eagle's attendant must have dashed around the curve of the game trail and straight into the path of the enormous animal.

Having missed the first object of its wrath, the rhinoceros did not bother to differentiate between Dawn and the Mun-Gatah. Instead, its horn had been lowered and snapped upwards with all its might. Taking him between the thighs, the solid mass of hard-packed fibres sank into the man's body. Blood gushed from the wound as he was thrown over the animal's head. Although he landed on and bounced helplessly from the beast's back, the rhinoceros did not attempt to turn.

127

Instead, it continued to rush straight ahead, shattering a way through the undergrowth as though the foliage did not exist.

Dawn looked at the man and knew that he was beyond any human aid. Then she glanced around in the hope of locating his sword. As its scabbard was empty, he must have been carrying the weapon. In which case, as it was nowhere to be seen, it must have left his hand when he was tossed and landed among the bushes. Concluding that trying to find it would be a waste of time, she turned and walked onwards.

On reaching the fringe of the bushes, after having had to wind about due to the vagaries of the trail, Dawn paused to survey her surroundings before emerging. She looked to the right without finding anything to disturb her. However, as her gaze turned in the opposite direction, she discovered that the smaller of the women and one of the men were sitting their zebras about two hundred yards away. They had either found a way through, or had passed around the end of the bushes and were now scanning the edge in search of her.

Deciding that she had not decoyed her pursuers far enough away from the injured Telonga hunter, Dawn ignored her first impulse to withdraw into the comparative safety of the bushes. Instead, she walked out in a cautious manner. It would, she hoped, lead the couple to believe that she was unaware of their presence. The land ahead was still fairly open. However, beyond a small stream which she suspected might be the one that had supplied the means to bandage At-Vee's sprained ankle, the trees began to grow more closely together.

"There she is!" shrieked the woman. "Mador! Elidor! She's between us!"

"Stupid bitch!" Dawn thought, as the excited words reached her ears.

Chanak was uttering a similar sentiment, although —because of his companion's relationship with the Protectress of the Quagga God—he too did not put it into words. What annoyed him was the fact that

Sabart's shout would do more than just warn the foreign girl that she had been seen. It would also bring the High Priest's adherents onto the scene. They had not yet come into sight at the other end of the bushes and, but for Sabart's stupidity, might not have appeared until after the quarry had been captured.

Acting as she believed the Mun-Gatahs would expect of her, Dawn started to run. She had already gained some ground on her pursuers. So she went at a swift lope which would allow her to carry on for a long distance, or to increase speed if necessary. Hearing the sound of hooves and voices to her right, she chanced a glance in that direction. At a somewhat greater distance than the small woman and her companion, the brunette and another of the men were turning from around the end of the bushes.

Coming to the stream, Dawn built up her speed and leapt across. On landing, she continued to run. Weaving through the trees, she found that she could hear enough to make it unnecessary to look back at her pursuers. They were coming closer, but not sufficiently so for her to feel any alarm. In fact, if the cursing which occasionally reached her ears meant anything, now they had passed over the stream, the men were finding increasing difficulty in moving through the denser growth.

Having covered about another quarter of a mile, Dawn decided that she had created enough of a diversion. The terrain was becoming more densely overgrown and she guessed that she must be approaching the transitory zone between the woodland and the jungle. If the Mun-Gatahs lost her, they might be disinclined to continue the search. Living as they did on the open plains, they could even be afraid of getting lost if they penetrated any deeper into such an alien environment. In which case, they would most likely take the easiest way out and return along their tracks. If so, they would miss finding any trace of her meeting with At-Vee and she would have achieved her purpose.

Fortune appeared to be continuing to smile on

Dawn. Ahead, a tree had started to fall for some reason. It had been prevented from doing so by its crown having become entangled with the foliage of a neighbour. Leaning at an angle, it offered her the means by which she could travel as she had been taught—and had frequently practiced—in her tomboy childhood. What was more, although at least some of her pursuers were fairly close, a glance to her rear informed her that she was hidden from their view. In which case, she ought to be able to make a complete disappearance.

Alert for shouts, or anything else that would suggest she had been seen, Dawn ran up the inclined trunk. She went with the agility of a cat, but was not sorry that she had left her bow and quiver of arrows with At-Vee. Useful as they undoubtedly would have been if it had come to a fight, they would have made climbing and the mode of progression that she was contemplating very difficult. On reaching the branches of the supporting tree without having heard anything to disturb her, she prepared to continue her flight in a way which she felt sure would baffle the Mun-Gatahs. Even if she could not go very far, she believed it would suffice for her needs.

As always when about to start travelling through the branches, Dawn found herself thinking with wry amusement of how this particular activity had invariably been portrayed in the fictitious movies about Tarzan. If she could only find a succession of conveniently positioned vines, everything would be so much easier. Unfortunately that mode of passage through the trees had never existed outside a movie production unit's sets.*

With the thought come and gone, for she would need all her wits about her, the girl ran along a sturdy branch until she felt it bending under her weight. While doing so, she studied the nearest tree and selected a

---

*At no time in his twenty-four biographical books on the life of Lord Greystoke does Edgar Rice Burroughs suggest that Tarzan made use of vines when traveling through the trees.

suitable place to alight. Then, making use of the
bough's springiness, she leapt forward. On arriving in
the next tree, she deftly regained her balance and
darted to its trunk. Mounting higher, she picked out a
limb which would allow her to reach the foliage of the
neighbouring tree.

Although effective in allowing Dawn to move without leaving tracks on the ground, her passage through
the lower terraces of the jungle was of necessity a noisy
process. She had to crash through the leaves, breaking
twigs and small branches to attain a safe point of arrival. So she stopped in the third tree and found a position from which she could see the ground.

From all appearances, the two parties had not yet
come together. While the smaller woman and her companion were already passing the partially fallen tree,
there was no sign of the second couple. Dawn found
that she could see the first pair and, although she could
not hear what they were saying, guessed that they had
been attracted by the noise she had been making as
she moved onwards through the branches. They were
staring upwards, paying more attention to the foliage
than the ground. The man had either lost, or discarded, his lance, for he no longer had it with him.
The woman was looking nervously upwards, alternat-
ing the scrutiny with glances darted from side to side
at the bushes and tree trunks.

Passing around the bole of the tree, Dawn found that
it was on the edge of a small clearing. Measuring the
distance to be crossed, she decided that she ought to be
able to leap over. There was a convenient, sturdy
branch that she could catch hold of and, by using simple brachiation, swing from it to a more secure perch.

After a moment's thought, the girl considered that
the chance might be worth taking. Once in the other
tree, she would give the distress call of a she-*Mangani*.
There was just a slight chance that Bunduki would
hear and identify it. In which case, he would come as
quickly as possible to her aid. Even if he did not, the
cry might serve a useful purpose. From the look of the

woman, she was already nervous. Hearing the far from pleasant scream emanating out of the foliage, she and her companions might be frightened into turning back.

Once again utilizing the resilience of the branch along which she was advancing as a means of added propulsion, Dawn threw herself forward and up as if diving from a spring board. As she was flying through the air, she thrust her arms ahead of her. Just before her hands—with the fingers bent and the thumbs tucked in out of the way—came into contact with the branch, she saw a slight movement on it.

It was a snake!

Dawn did not have any unreasoning fear of reptiles, but she had a very sensible caution regarding some of them. She knew that out of the 2,300 species of living snakes, divided into twelve families, only about a third were poisonous to a greater or lesser degree. Of those which were venomous, a mere seven-per-cent were capable of causing death to a human being. However, despite the odds favouring the snake being harmless, she felt disinclined to take the chance. Nor could she prevent the involuntary withdrawal of her left hand, which would have descended on to the reptile.

Although the girl's right fingers hooked over the branch clear of the snake, she had been thrown off balance. Swinging by the one arm, she felt her grasp slipping. Then her head struck the limb a glancing blow, but it was sufficient to stun her. Losing her hold, she toppled into the denser foliage below her. It began to bend under her limp and unresisting weight.

Down and down Dawn went. Although vaguely aware of the predicament she was in, her mind refused to function. In a way, her dazed state was fortunate. If she had tried to halt her progress, she could easily have made things worse. Instead, she was tumbling limply and with her body yielding rather than trying to resist when it came up against the branches.

Dropping the final ten feet, the girl was lucky in that she came down on a thick layer of leaves and moss. Being so relaxed, the worse effects of the fall were broken. For all that, her landing jarred all the breath from her body. After a brief period when everything appeared to explode into a brilliant burst of colours, blackness descended like a cloud over her and she lay still.

Having heard the commotion as Dawn fell and noticing the silence that followed it, Sabart and Chanak advanced in a wary and watchful fashion. As yet, Elidor and Mador had not caught up with them. Nor did they offer to wait until the High Priest's adherents could do so. Chanak had discarded his lance soon after crossing the stream, having found it more of a hindrance while passing through the denser growth, especially as he wanted to keep ahead of the other two. So he was riding with his sword unsheathed and in his right hand.

For her part, Sabart was perturbed and not a little afraid. Ever since the eerie cry had arisen from the depths of the bushes, followed by sounds such as a rhinoceros made when it was attacking and the scream of a man—the eagle's attendant, Shanu, most likely—in mortal agony, she had been experiencing a sensation of superstitious dread. Nor had it grown less at the events which had followed.

According to Chanak, the foreign girl's tracks had disappeared in a way that suggested she had climbed the inclined trunk of a tree. However, there had been no sign of her among the foliage. Instead, they had heard noises from the branches of the nearby trees which had been suggestive of those made by a monkey leaping from one to another—except that something larger and heavier was responsible for them.

Remembering the various stories she had heard about the "Hairy People" and being uncomfortably aware that she was approaching what was said to be their domain, Sabart was troubled by her thoughts. She could not forget how Tomlu had been killed, with the arrow sunk so deeply into his chest *through* his breastplate.

No ordinary human being could have done such a thing!

What if——?

"There she is!"

Chanak's excited comment cut through Sabart's uneasy sequence of thoughts. Looking in the direction which he was indicating, she let out a sigh of relief and urged her *banar-gatah* forward with a greater willingness than she had up to now been displaying.

Crossing the small clearing, Sabart and Chanak halted the zebras. After a quick glance around, they dismounted and stood over Dawn's unconscious body. They could hear Elidor and Mador approaching and exchanged delighted glances.

"*We've* got her, Chanak!" Sabart enthused, unaware that a similar sentiment was being expressed by her rival.

Elidor and Mador had not made any special effort to catch up with the Protectress's supporters. Instead, they had been content to follow at a distance which would have allowed them to retire if the foreign girl had led them into an ambush. They had closed the gap somewhat, due to the other two slowing down when they reached the place where Dawn had taken to the trees.

"May the Quagga God curse them!" Elidor spat out, glaring furiously through the undergrowth and across the clearing. "They've caught the foreign bitch!"

"Dryaka won't be pleased when we go back and say Charole's got her," Mador answered, scowling malevolently and making what his companion considered to be an understatement.

"I wouldn't want to have to go back and tell him," Elidor declared, bringing her *banar-gatah* to a halt. "And *I've* no intention of doing it."

In the clearing by Dawn's body, Chanak nodded his agreement with Sabart's statement. Then he turned to his zebra. He opened the left side saddlebag and removed a long rawhide thong. Going to Dawn and kneeling at her side, he rolled her onto her stomach.

After pulling her hands behind her back, ignoring her groan and feeble movements as she struggled to regain consciousness, he used the thong to secure her wrists. Having done so, he drew the Randall knife from its sheath.

Although Chanak's primary intention had been to disarm the girl, the look and feel of the weapon attracted his attention. He did not realize that he was holding an example of what Judge Roy S. Tinney, secretary of the American Academy of Arms, had described as "a refined and perfected Bowie," or that the eight-inch-long, clip-pointed blade was hand-made from the finest Swedish tool steel. However, he could tell that it might be as special and unusual as the bow and arrows with which she had dispatched Charole's eagle and Tomlu.

"*This* is mine!" the man stated, showing the knife to Sabart.

"Charole will see that you get it when we deliver this bitch to her," the woman answered, stirring the weakly struggling and groaning girl with her left toe. "I can hardly wait to see what she'll do to her."

Being so full of themselves and absorbed in their respective sources of delight—Sabart because Dawn had been captured, and Chanak because he had gained almost certain possession of something which he knew was very special—two very important matters had slipped right out of their minds.

When sending the party to capture Dawn, Dryaka had deliberately avoided any mention of the importance that he attached to also obtaining her bow and arrows. For all that, her captors ought to have given thought to the fact that she was no longer carrying them.

Of infinitely greater importance to them personally was the fact that neither was giving any consideration to how their rivals might react when learning that they had achieved their purpose.

The latter omission was to cost them dearly.

Sabart was the first to become aware that they were being remiss in their behaviour. Hearing the sound of hooves behind her, she turned with the intention of displaying her triumph to her rival. What she saw drove all thoughts of enjoyment and satisfaction from her head. One glance was all she needed to realize that she and her companion were in grave danger.

While Elidor and Mador had entered the clearing side by side, only the man was mounted. That the woman was on foot of her own free will was shown by the thing which she was carrying in her right hand. That, and the way in which Mador was sitting on his *banar-gatah* gave a grim warning that they did not intend to surrender their claim to the prisoner, despite her having fallen into their rivals' hands.

"Chanak!" Sabart screamed, sending her right hand across towards the hit of her sword. "Look behi——!"

Darting forward, Elidor drew back and snapped forward her right arm. The spear which she had drawn from its retaining loops on the skirt of her saddle left her hand and flashed across the clearing. Its point struck Sabart just below the left breast and impaled her before she could even start to draw the sword or to attempt any kind of evasion.

With her warning ending in a shriek of agony, the stricken woman spun around and bumped into Chanak. It could not have happened at a worse moment. Having glanced around, he too had appreciated the peril and was preparing to counter it. He was thrusting himself erect, letting Dawn's knife drop as he reached for the sword—a more familiar weapon—that he had sheathed before securing their prisoner. Rebounding after having knocked her companion off balance, Sabart clutched ineffectually at the spear's handle and fell alongside Dawn.

As the spear was leaving Elidor's hand, a touch from Mador's heels gave his well-trained *banar-gatah* the signal which it had been expecting since its rider had lowered his lance to the "ready" position. The animal bounded forward, guided by knee pressure rather than control from the reins held in the man's left hand. It built up speed rapidly, making for what its instincts said was the object of its master's attentions.

Watching Chanak staggering from the collision with Sabart, Mador let out a hiss of triumph. The mishap had put the Protectress's adherent at his mercy. However, he knew better than to take chances with a man as experienced as Chanak was in fighting on foot against a mounted, lance-carrying opponent. With the *banar-gatah* carrying him into striking distance, he aligned his weapon at a downwards angle.

Chanak recognized his terrible predicament, but could do nothing to avert it. Nor did he have any false hopes about surviving the encounter.

While a Mun-Gatah's breastplate would turn aside the usual kind of arrows with which the wearer was brought into conflict, their own lances were a very different proposition. At the end of the nine foot shaft of male bamboo, the head had a twelve-inches-long, diamond-section steel blade that was two-and-a-half-inches at its widest and tapered to an acute point. It was retained in position by a pair of steel languets some three feet long which extended down the pole and were secured by six screws on each side.* All in all, it made a very deadly weapon and was one which the Mun-Gatah warriors had brought to the peak of efficiency.

Before Chanak could regain his equilibrium, the point of Mador's lance met the centre of his chest. The High Priest's supporter had the rear end of the shaft tucked under his right arm and was pressing it tight against his ribs. In addition to his hand grasping the shaped grip at the point of balance, greater firmness and security was achieved from the rawhide loop that was attached just above it and encircled his wrist.

Aided by the *banar-gatah's* onrushing impetus, the lance's head cut through Chanak's breastplate and into

*The languets of the British Army's 1848 Pattern lance, which has similar dimensions, were secured by only five screws.

the flesh below. The impact threw him backwards and form his feet. Turning his hand as his victim went down and his mount rushed by, Mador released his hold and slipped his wrist from the loop. Reining the *banar-gatah* around, he drew his sword and, when the turn was completed, sprang from the saddle. He knew there would be no need for the second weapon. Pinned to the ground by the lance, Chanak lay supine with his limbs flailing spasmodically. Even that movement ended before Mador reached him.

"She's ours now, Mador!" Elidor stated delightedly, placing her foot on Sabart's lifeless body as an aid in retrieving her spear. "We'll have to do something about Stafak, though."

"We'll give him the same as these two," Mador stated. "Then, when we get back, we'll say that we were separated and pretend to be surprised that they aren't back."

"She could spoil that for us," Elidor warned, indicating the still unconscious girl.

"Not if she doesn't know that's happened," Mador pointed out. "Take them and their *banar-gatahs* into the woods where she'll not be able to see them. Then go and kill Stafak. I'll look after her."

"Make sure that *look* is all you do," Elidor advised, knowing the man. "Dryaka wanted her for himself."

CHAPTER TWELVE

I'll Break Every Bone In Your Body

"BUNDUKI! Bunduki! Help!"

Standing on the crotch of the tree into which he had climbed to make preparations for spending the night, the blond giant dropped the leaves he had gathered on to the pile of branches as he heard Joar-Fane's terror-filled voice screaming the words.

Having heard Dawn's distress call, without having realized that it was she who had given it, Bunduki had—much to Joar-Fane's annoyance—insisted upon resuming their journey. He had reduced her irritation by explaining to her his plans for ensuring their safety from prowling carnivores during the hours of darkness. Accepting the situation with what good grace she could muster, she had apparently consoled herself by considering and anticipating the pleasures which she felt sure lay ahead. Certainly, she had been cheerful enough as she had walked along at his side.

By the time the sun had started to set, Bunduki and Joar-Fane had been approaching the more open woodland. Completely unaware that Dawn had been taken captive by the Mun-Gatahs, although he still had the subconscious belief that she was somewhere to the north-west and might be in danger, the blond giant had realized that trying to continue the search after night had fallen would be futile. So he had selected a tree which met his requirements and, while Joar-Fane had taken the remains of the capybara's leg to wash it in a stream they had passed a short while earlier, he had set about making the kind of a bed that chimpanzees and the *Mangani* used in the branches of trees.

Looking downwards, Bunduki found that the undergrowth prevented him from discovering the cause of Joar-Fane's cry for help. So he did not waste time in making useless speculation. Instead, he grabbed the vine which he had cut so that its end was dangling to the ground in order to help the girl attain their bedplatform. Going down hand over hand at considerable speed, he let go and dropped when certain he could do so without risk of injury. Although his bow and arrows were lying at the foot of the tree, he did not pause to gather them up. As soon as he alighted, he started to run towards the point from which he had last heard the girl.

Bunduki did not know what to expect as he sprinted through the bushes. Nor was there anything to supply a clue. After her first shouted words, Joar-Fane had been silent. Nor had he heard any other sounds that might have accounted for her state of alarm. It was possible that she had fallen foul of *Bul-Mok's* family, or another group of *Mangani*. Or it might be some kind of animal which was stalking her. No matter what it was, there was nothing to suggest that it had caught or was attacking her.

Passing around the edge of a clump of bushes, the blond giant received the answer.

At the far side of the clearing, Joar-Fane was standing with her back against the trunk of a tree. She was grasping a thick piece of a branch in the manner of a club and glaring at the tall, shapely, black-haired woman who was stalking arrogantly towards her. Nor was the woman alone. There were three men present. The largest was standing with his back to the blond giant, watching Joar-Fane and the woman. Advancing along the edges of the clearing, the other two were positioned to cut off the girl if she tried to run either way.

All of the quartet were dressed and armed in much the same manner. While the woman's hair had no covering, the men had on leather helmets decorated on each side by the embossed head of a horse—or a zebra. All wore one piece, short, white tunics—the woman's being sleeveless—and had a sword shaped like the *gladius* of a Roman soldier in a scabbard on the left side of the belt. They had sandals on their feet and leather greaves protected their shins.

Ground hitched by their dangling one-piece reins, the four saddled animals among the trees at the left side of the clearing supplied the blond giant with a clue to the quartet's identity. He had already suspected that they might be the party sent by the Mun-Gatahs' People-Taker to recapture Joar-Fane. There was a white garment of some kind hanging from each saddle's cantle, but he did not waste time in trying to decide what they might be.

"Watch her, Latica!" called the biggest man, drawing Bunduki's attention from the zebras. He was clearly more amused than perturbed by the girl's threatening attitude. "She might be an Amazon in disguise."

"I'll 'Amazon' her!" the woman answered, without looking back or offering to draw her sword. "Put that stick down, damn you, or I'll break every bone in your body."

"You try it and see what I'll do!" Joar-Fane replied spiritedly, seeing the blond giant at the edge of the clearing and wanting to prevent the Mun-Gatahs from becoming aware of his presence. "I'm not afraid of you."

Having reached his conclusion regarding the identity of the quartet, Bunduki was taking advantage of their preoccupation with the girl and was moving forward. Noticing that she had seen him, he was pleased by the way she was acting. She was behaving in a much braver and more intelligent manner than he would have expected.

Remembering what Joar-Fane had told him about the Mun-Gatahs, the blond giant doubted whether he could save her by peaceful means. Nor, if he was correct in his assumption of where he had been transported by his unknown saviours, could he follow the dictates

of the civilized society in which he had been born and
raised. He must be ready to fight and kill if he wanted
to survive and rescue the girl.

Accepting that there was no other choice, Bunduki ran towards the largest of the men. His bare feet
made little sound on the springy turf and the man,
who almost matched him in size and bulk, was not
aware of his approach. That was all to the good and
the big blond hoped to turn it to his advantage. If he
could take the man by surprise and use him as a hostage, it might still be possible to avoid bloodshed.

"You're up against a fierce one th——!" the warrior at the right commenced.

The words died away as the speaker became aware
of a figure coming from the bushes ahead of him.
Dressed in a jaguar-skin loincloth, the newcomer had
his right leg bandaged by leaves and was limping along
using a stout spear as a crutch. In his left hand, he held
a weapon of a kind the Mun-Gatah had never seen. He
looked like a Telonga, except that those with whom
the People-Taker's party had come into contact were
never armed, nor so muscular.

Studying the newcomer's black hair, dark skin and
Polynesian features, Bunduki assumed that he belonged to Joar-Fane's people. However, despite the
thing like a *czákan* that he was carrying, his injured
leg would reduce his effectiveness in a fight.

"An *armed* Telonga, as I live and breathe!" the warrior on the right shouted derisively and looked behind
him. "I'll need your he——!" Once again he did not
complete a speech. Instead, he started to swing around
and his right hand went to the hilt of the sword as he
shouted, "Behind you!"

Hearing and seeing the change in his companion's
words and behaviour, the third male member of the
party glanced back. What he saw caused him to duplicate the second's actions. The woman threw a look to
her rear and half-turned, reaching for her sword. Unaware of At-Vee's arrival on the scene, as he was coming from behind her, Joar-Fane let out a yell and,

swinging the club above her head in both hands, sprang forward.

Seeing first one, then the other warrior turning and preparing to arm themselves, Bunduki abandoned his ideas of trying to take the nearest man as a hostage. The other two appeared to be devoting their attentions to him and ignoring the newcomer. Nor, if the painful way in which he was moving meant anything, would the Telonga be of much use. Certainly he could not come quickly enough to be of assistance. So Bunduki put aside his original notion of giving the largest man a chance to turn and fight. The odds were sufficiently high without him adding to them by pandering to ideals of fair play and chivalry. He knew that such sentiments would not be accorded to him if their positions were reversed.

Increasing his speed, Bunduki hurled himself into the air in such a way that his body was almost horizontal. His left shoulder rammed into the centre of the man's back. Struck by the full force of the blond giant's two hundred and twenty pound frame, the Mun-Gatah was knocked from his feet. Nor did it end there. There was a sharp crack, followed by a scream of pain, as his spine snapped.

Going down with the stricken man, Bunduki rolled clear and started to rise. His right hand flashed across to close on the ivory hilt of the bowie knife, sliding it from its sheath. There was not a second to lose. Already the two warriors were converging upon him.

Alerted by Joar-Fane's yell, the woman looked back at her. Finding that the girl was attempting to attack her, she let out an angry snort. Swivelling around swiftly, she stepped forward and, before Joar-Fane could bring the weapon down, lashed around her right arm. Caught at the side of the head by a powerful backhand blow, the little Telonga went spinning. The club flew from her hand and she measured her length, dazed and helpless, on the ground.

Still in the process of rising, Bunduki analyzed the situation with great rapidity. There was, he decided, one thing in his favour. The man to his left was much closer than the other warrior and showed no sign of slowing down. Therefore they could not launch a concerted attack.

Wanting to gain the acclaim that would accrue from avenging what he guessed had been a fatal assault on his leader, the first warrior had no intention of taking the sensible course of co-operating with his companion. Instead, he bounded onwards at an increased pace. Arriving within range, he launched a savage downwards chop with his sword at the side of the blond giant's neck.

Thrusting himself erect, Bunduki held the bowie knife with its blade projecting in front of his thumb and forefinger. It was a grip that allowed him to utilize the weapon to the best advantage, permitting a cut, thrust, or backhand slash with equal facility.

Bringing the knife across, the blond giant let the flat of the blade meet and sweep aside the Mun-Gatah's sword. Then, disengaging his weapon, he delivered a devastatingly effective counter attack. Hissing to the right, the knife—which had an edge as sharp as a barber's razor—passed under the man's chin. The steel sliced inwards, laying open the Mun-Gatah's throat to the bone with a force that twisted him aside. The sword fell from his fingers and they rose to clutch at the hideous, blood-spurting mortal wound. Collapsing to his knees, he fell forward on to his face.

Seeing the second of his party struck down by the big blond did not deter the last of the warriors. He continued to rush towards Bunduki and was so close that he felt sure he could make his attack before there would be any chance of evasion or reprisals.

Alert to the danger, the blond giant prepared to defend himself. He saw that the man was adopting almost identical tactics to those of the first assailant. Once again, the attack came in the form of a round-house swing. Except that this time it was travelling horizontally rather than at a downwards angle.

Pivoting to face his assailant, Bunduki bent his right

knee and thrust his left leg backwards in a long stride. Doing so caused him to sink below the arc of the sword's swing. Even as it went over his head, stirring his hair it passed so close, he turned the knuckles of his right hand uppermost. Out drove the bowie knife in an almost classic lunge. Carried onwards by his momentum, the man paid the price of failure. Spiking its clip point into his stomach, the bowie's blade sank almost to its brass lugged guard.

While dealing with the third male Mun-Gatah, Bunduki did not forget the woman. Even as his knife was entering the man's body, he looked to find out what she was doing. Like her companions, she appeared to consider him a greater danger than the Telonga hunter. That was true. Due to the "putting away," the People-Taker and his escort had only come into contact with the placid, unresisting male members of the Telonga nation. So she was discounting the Telonga hunter as a serious factor—as the two warriors had— and felt that he could be disposed of easily enough once the blond giant had been killed.

With the latter thought in mind, and ignoring the Telonga hunter and the motionless girl, the woman advanced across the clearing towards Bunduki. Judging from the way she held her sword she might prove as dangerous as either of the warriors, or possibly more so if she had taken a warning from the results of their rash behaviour and was skilled with the weapon. Bunduki straightened his right leg and, driving himself erect, he swung the stricken man to the left in a way that ripped the bowie's blade through flesh and freed it.

Practically disembowelled and letting go of his sword, the dying man tottered in a half circle until he was facing the woman. She stared in horror at the intestines which were oozing from the gaping tear in his stomach and came to an involuntary halt. Then, as she watched him crumpling like a rag doll that had had its stuffing removed, her nerve failed her. Instead of continuing with her advance, she fled at an angle that would take her to the waiting zebras but would at the same time keep her well beyond the reach of the blond giant who had felled all of her companions.

Throwing a glance at Joar-Fane, Bunduki was relieved to see that she was moving and that there was no blood to suggest she had been stabbed. The hunter was hurrying towards her with his face showing mingled anxiety and pain. Feeling sure that the girl was not seriously hurt, the blond giant started to go towards the woman.

Having no desire for further killing, Bunduki did not want to catch and deal with Latica. Nor did he wish to be encumbered by a prisoner. He had something else in mind. Being an excellent horseman, he was hoping to gain possession of at least one of the zebras. He felt sure that he could ride it. In which case, it could prove very useful in his search for his adoptive cousin.

On reaching the animals, having seen that the blond giant was following her and misinterpreting his motives, the woman acted with panic-induced speed. Dropping her sword instead of sheathing it, she grabbed the reins of her *ocha-gatah*. Taking them over its head, she caught hold of the saddlehorn and vaulted on to its back. Almost as soon as her rump hit the leather, she sent her mount bounding forward without as much as a glance at the dead companions she was leaving behind.

Deciding that the woman was too frightened to come back, Bunduki hurried towards the three remaining zebras. Although they appeared to have been made a little restless by her hurried departure, none of them showed any signs of bolting. Studying them as he was cleaning the blood from his knife and returning it to its sheath, he unconsciously matched Dawn's summation regarding their physical conformation and possible relationship to wild zebras. One reminded him of the subspecies *Equus Grevy,* but the other two had the colours and striping of *Equus Burchelli.*

A glance across the clearing reassured Bunduki that Joar-Fane had not been seriously injured. The hunter was kneeling somewhat awkwardly, holding her in his arms and she was behaving much as she had after the blond giant had saved her from the *Mangani.*

Pleased to find that the girl was unharmed and obviously on good terms with the man, Bunduki turned his attention to the zebras. Going to the *banar-gatah,* although he did not identify it by its Mun-Gatah name, he acted as he would if he had been approaching a strange horse. Speaking in a low, soothing voice and avoiding any sudden movements, he reached out slowly with his right hand. The *banar-gatah* snorted, tossed its head, then calmed and allowed him to stroke its sleek neck.

With friendly relations established, the blond giant examined the *banar-gatah's* furnishings. The saddle had a low horn, double girths and wide, iron-bound wooden stirrups much like a Texas range rig. There was a throwing spear in two loops attached to the left side of its skirt, suggesting that its rider mounted on that flank. The bridle was made so that, by unbuckling the straps, the bit, snaffle and reins could be removed but the head-stall—from which a coiled tether-rope was dangling—would remain in place.

There was, Bunduki decided, something strange about the three animals' equipment. It was not the fact that the Mun-Gatahs had stirrups. These had been invented in China about 400 B.C. and were in widespread use throughout the known world by 700 A.D. What puzzled him was the way in which the rigs had been manufactured. While the gear on the other two zebras suggested ownership by persons of a lower social standing, there was a similarity between them that was rare in hand-made products. Obviously the Mun-Gatahs had very skilful craftsmen to produce such good quality work. Yet it almost seemed that they had been using modern machinery and techniques; but that was impossible.

Turning his attention to the white garment that was rolled and passed through two loops on the cantle of the saddle, Bunduki drew it out. It had the smooth, silky, shiny appearance of the wool, cotton, or acetate rayon fabrics known as "sharkskin." Opening it out, he found it to be a kind of sleeveless over-tunic with a cowl for the head. Emblazoned on its front was a remarkably well drawn and coloured illustration of a rearing, horse-like animal. After a moment's study, he decided that it was supposed to be a quagga such as had been extinct for many years. He was fascinated, not only by the portrayal of a long deceased kind of creature but at the way the design was imprinted on the material. The latter exceeded anything he had seen produced by primitive people.

With his curiosity aroused, the blond giant hung the garment over the *banar-gathah's* saddle and picked up the woman's sword. He found it both interesting and puzzling. While the metal of its blade could not compare with the Swedish high carbon tool steel from which his Smithsonian bowie had been created, it was a much better temper than he had expected. What was more, the design and finish of the weapon suggested a high standard of workmanship. So much so that it, like the garment and the zebras' equipment, might have been produced by machines rather than hand. Yet nothing he had seen about the Mun-Gatahs had implied that they belonged to a race that was capable of designing, manufacturing or even operating a piece of sophisticated modern machinery. It was, of course, possible that they bought, looted or traded their weapons from a more advanced nation.

Once more, the urgency of Bunduki's desire to find his adoptive cousin caused him to turn his thoughts from a puzzling aspect. His handling of the *banar-gatah* had so far been successful. Realizing that the same might not apply when he attempted to ride it, he decided to take precautions against losing them all. Dropping the sword and opening out the tether ropes of the two *ocha-gatahs,* he fastened them to stout branches of the bushes. With the spare animals secured and prevented from escaping, even if the other should throw him and bolt, he took its reins and led it into the clearing.

On his return, the blond giant found Joar-Fane and the man kneeling facing each other and talking. Suddenly, the girl gave a gasp and turned her head in his direction.

"Bunduki!" Joar-Fane gasped. "At-Vee has met Dawn———."

"Where is she?" the blond giant demanded, striding forward.

"I don't know," At-Vee admitted, then explained the circumstances of his meeting with, and separation from, Dawn. "I heard the call of a 'Hairy Woman,' then the sound of a rhinoceros attacking and a scream———."

"Was it Dawn?" Bunduki growled.

"I don't think so," At-Vee replied. "It sounded like a man. But she hasn't come back, nor have I heard anything else until Joar-Fane called for help."

"Where did you hear the call of the 'Hairy Woman'?" Bunduki inquired. "Which direction, I mean."

"There," At-Vee answered, pointing to the west. "It was a long way off, but not in the jungle."

Looking in the direction indicated by the hunter, Bunduki decided to try and make contact with his adoptive cousin by the same means which he had employed shortly after waking that morning. If she was in the vicinity, she ought to be able to identify his voice. Provided she could do so, she would respond and guide him to her. Without thinking to warn his companions, he threw back his head and thundered out the challenge roar of a bull *Mangani*.

Startled exclamations burst from Joar-Fane and At-Vee, but the effect of the awesome bellow was even more marked in the reactions of the zebras. Letting out snorts of alarm, they all began to rear. Before the *banar-gatah* could bolt, Bunduki sprang forward and caught hold of its reins. He brought its wildly pawing forelegs back to earth and hung on grimly, being determined not to lose such a valuable means of transport. While doing so, he also tried to listen for any answering call from Dawn. A bull *Mangani* replied from far off in the jungle, but the sound he was hoping to hear did not reach him.

Having brought the *banar-gatah* back under control and looked around to make sure that the two *ochagatahs* had neither torn free from the bushes nor injured themselves in their attempts to do so, the blond giant turned to Joar-Fane and At-Vee.

"Did you hear anything?" Bunduki asked.

"Only the 'Hairy Man' in the jungle," At-Vee answered, realizing what the big blond had been trying to do. "Dawn hasn't answered."

"Perhaps she didn't hear you, Bunduki," Joar-Fane suggested. "She might be too far away."

"She might," the blond giant agreed.

"Or they could have captured her and won't let her reply," At-Vee offered. "I should never have let her go——."

"From what I know about Dawn, you couldn't have stopped her once she'd made up her mind," Bunduki replied. "I'll have to go and look for her."

Even as the blond giant spoke, he glanced at the rapidly darkening sky. Any search that he commenced would be of short duration before the coming of night brought it to a halt. So he decided that he would have to leave it until daybreak. The decision did not come easily. While either of the possibilities mentioned by his companions could explain Dawn's failure to respond to his call, there was another alternative. Much as he hated the thought, his adoptive cousin could be dead.

CHAPTER THIRTEEN

Let Me Make Her Talk, Lord Dryaka

SITTING astride the *grar-gatah* that had belonged to the eagle's attendant, with her wrists secured by a set of rawhide hobbles—the metal swivel connecting link of which was fastened to the saddlehorn—and ankles tied to the stirrups, Dawn Drummond Clayton surveyed her surroundings with considerable misgivings.

Leading their captive's mount by its tether rope, Elidor rode along oozing pride and arrogance. She was delighted by the interest her party's arrival was causing as they passed through the Mun-Gatahs' hunting camp. Displaying an equal satisfaction, Mador and the second male warrior rode one on either side of their tawny-haired prisoner.

On returning to full consciousness the previous afternoon, Dawn had become aware that she was in a terrible predicament and had sought for a way out of it. Only Mador had been with her when she had regained the use of her faculties. However, although she had been ready to resist most strenuously if he had attempted to take advantage of her hands being bound behind her back, she had realized the futility of trying to attack him. So she had not attempted to. Instead, she had remained passive in the hope that she might lull him into a sense of over-confidence thus offering her an opportunity to escape. Before it could happen, Elidor and the second of the High Priest's male adherents had returned. They had been leading the *grar-gatah* and, after changing Dawn's bonds for the hobbles, the men had lifted her onto its saddle and fastened

151

her there. With that done, they had led her back in the direction from which they had come.

At first, while awaiting whatever might be in store for her, Dawn had been puzzled by the absence of her original pair of pursuers. Noticing two patches of freshly spilled blood on the ground, she guessed what had happened but kept her thoughts to herself. That had been a wise decision. Wanting to avoid having their lies exposed by the girl when they reached the hunting camp, Elidor and Mador had removed the bodies and their victims' mounts before she had recovered. Then the woman had gone and disposed of Charole's third supporter while collecting the last member of her party.

Although Dawn had had no difficulty in sitting the *grar-gatah,* its gait being similar to that of an ordinary riding horse, she had contrived to hide the fact from her captors. By pretending to have no knowledge of equestrian matters, she had managed to delay them and reduce the speed at which they were travelling. Night had found them on the plains and they made camp on the banks of a small stream.

While lifting Dawn from the saddle, the men's hands had wandered over her private parts. However, neither had attempted to go any further than feeling her body. Despite her relief at not having been sexually assaulted, she had found the omission disturbing. To her way of thinking, it had suggested she might be being reserved for some other fate.

Dawn had heard and recognized Bunduki's challenge roar, but had known that to try and answer would be inadvisable. If she had made the attempt, she would have been quickly, and, in all probability, painfully silenced. So she remained silent. She noticed how nervous the awesome bellow had made the zebras, even though it had been a long way off.

Knowing that Bunduki was searching for her had heartened Dawn. She had deduced that he might have been guided by a similar subconscious impulse to that which had brought her to the woodland. However, she had accepted that there was little likelihood of him finding her that night. Even if he should meet At-Vee and learn what had happened, he could not follow her tracks in the dark.

At sunrise, after having spent an uncomfortable night, Dawn had been given a meal of what she had guessed was the Mun-Gatahs' equivalent of *biltong*. Then she was placed on the *grar-gatah* and the journey was resumed. She had continued with her delaying tactics and had contrived to watch their back trail without making her interest in it obvious to her captors. Unfortunately, she had seen nothing to even suggest that Bunduki was following her tracks.

Shortly after noon, the party came into sight of the Mun-Gatahs' hunting camp. It was situated in the bottom of a large hollow and on the banks of a lake. Studying the way that the camp was laid out, Dawn had formed conclusions which were aided by the various comments she had heard passed between her captors. From what they had said, the nation was divided in its loyalties between the man and woman whom she had seen and spoken with at the edge of the chasm. Nor had there been any doubt as to which faction the trio supported.

The camp had been set up in the form of an open ended square. On the left and right sides, the tents grew in size until the far ones were of the pavilion type. The third side, which backed on to the lake, consisted of two more large pavilions with several smaller tents between them and the water. Watched over by youngsters wearing one piece white tunics, the majority of the party's zebras were grazing near the camp. However, several mounts were standing saddled outside various tents. Lances, with pennants flying, were thrust into the ground alongside the animals. Few of the men wore breastplates and only the woman showed any evidence of which factions they supported. Those whose were adherents of the Protectress of the Quagga God followed Charole's style of footwear. The supporters of the High Priest either wore greaves, or sandals of the slip-on variety.

Darting a look towards the pavilion on the left side, Elidor was disappointed to find that Charole was not coming from it. She did not doubt that the Protectress had been told of her arrival and she had been looking forward to flaunting her success. Sniffing in mingled annoyance and derision over Charole's failure to appear, the woman guided her captive to the right and stopped alongside the High Priest's quagga stallion.

Having been told that his party were returning, Dryaka strode majestically from his quarters. He had removed his breastplate and his helmet, exposing short-cropped black hair that was turning grey at the temples. He wore the usual white tunic, but with an illustration of a rearing quagga emblazoned on its chest. Halting just outside the pavilion, he gazed at Dawn with very evidence of satisfaction. Then he threw a glance across to the Protectress's temporary dwelling. Even as he noted that she had not come to the entrance, a thought struck him. His head swivelled back to the riders, going from one to another. His expression of triumph faded as he failed to see Dawn's bow and arrows.

"We've brought the foreign bitch as you told us, Lord Dryaka," Elidor announced, but she was puzzled and uneasy at the evidence of the High Priest's displeasure.

Before any more could be said the four members of the Council of Elders, who were on the hunt, emerged in pairs from their respective tents. Tall, bulky men with shoulder long white hair, they had on white toga-like garments that carried the rampant quagga insignia.

"So this is the foreign woman, Dryaka," said Hulkona, the senior Elder. He nodded his approval. "She will make a worthy sacrifice for the Quagga God."

"Where are Sabart and the others?" asked one of the second pair who was related to Charole and was hardly able to conceal his resentment that the High Priest's party had brought in the prisoner.

"Aren't they back yet?" Mador inquired, with such

sincerity that he might have been speaking the truth. "We separated when we lost her tracks. After we'd caught her, we called, but they didn't come and join us."

Although Dawn was momentarily tempted to tell what she suspected, she decided to keep quiet. Her suspicions might be of more use later. So she sat without speaking and awaited developments.

"Did you see any more of her people, Mador?" the High Priest put in, guessing that there might be considerably more to the story than had been told.

"No, Lord Dryaka," the man replied. "Perhaps Chanak has and is following them to see if he can capture more of them."

"It's possible," Dryaka conceded. "Bring her inside, I want to question her—if I may, my lords?"

"She's your prisoner," Hulkona answered, but he noticed that the request for permission had come almost as an afterthought. "Care for her well, *Lord* Dryaka."

"I will," the High Priest assured the Elder, for he could sense a warning in the last sentence. "Bring her inside."

Dismounting as the Elders walked away, Mador and the other man went to the *grar-gatah*. They liberated the girl's feet, then Mador removed the thong which had passed from the link of the hobbles to the saddle-horn. Before either man could make a move to lift her down, Dawn swung her right leg forward and above her mount's head. Freeing her left foot from the stirrup, she jumped to the ground. Remembering how awkward she had acted previously, Elidor let out a hiss of annoyance.

"Where is her knife?" the High Priest demanded, having watched Dawn's actions with interest, and noticed the empty sheath.

"I have it, my lord," Mador answered reluctantly, returning to his *banar-gatah* and opening the saddle-bag in which he had concealed the weapon.

"Take her inside, Elidor," Dryaka commanded, accepting the knife and finding, as he had expected, that it was of very high quality. "See to your mounts, Mador."

Swinging from her *banar-gatah's* saddle, the woman stalked forward. Catching Dawn by the left arm, she pulled at it with the intention of forcing the girl to enter the pavilion. For a moment, Dawn considered taking advantage of the opportunity to make a reprisal against Elidor. Prudence dictated against it. While she did not doubt that she could render Elidor *hors-de-combat,* the men, or some of the women who were hovering nearby, would quickly subdue her. So she allowed herself to be guided roughly into the entrance.

Dawn found that she had been hustled into the main section of the large tent. A padded mat of what appeared to be silk covered the ground. There were several large cushions scattered on it and a low, long table was placed parallel to the rear wall.

Receiving a push in the back, Dawn staggered forward a few steps and almost fell. She managed to remain on her feet and came to a halt in the centre of the floor. Turning angrily, she glared at Elidor. Then her eyes went to Dryaka. The High Priest had followed them inside and he was standing examining the Randall knife with obvious interest.

"It's very good, isn't it, my lord?" Elidor remarked, following in the direction that Dawn was looking. "Their 'Suppliers' give them better weapons than we get."

"Where are her bow and arrows?" Dryaka demanded, lowering the knife to his side.

"Her bow——?" Elidor began and an expression of perturbation came to her face. Suddenly she remembered the High Priest's interest in the arrows which had killed the eagle and Tomlu. She also realized what had caused Dryaka's annoyance when they had brought in the captive. "She—She must have thrown them away so she could run faster when she saw us coming."

An angry snort burst from the High Priest and, for a moment, he was on the point of striking the woman. He controlled his inclination with an effort, but his temper was not made any sweeter by the knowledge that he was partly to blame for the failure to gain possession of the girl's bow and arrows. Because of his desire to avoid letting Charole's supporters know how badly he wanted the weapons, he had not mentioned them when sending the party to hunt for Dawn. He had hoped that, if his adherents caught the girl, they would have sufficient sense to bring all her arms to him.

While Elidor and the two men were *banar-gatah* riders, they held their ranks by virtue of fighting ability rather than intelligence. That was one of the reasons why Dryaka considered Elidor an ideal replacement for Charole, whom he had helped to attain the position of Protectress of the Quagga God and who had subsequently proved too strong willed and clever to remain subservient to his will. Believing that Elidor would be more amenable and less ambitious, he had no wish to alienate her. So he decided to transfer his annoyance elsewhere.

"Where did you leave your bow and arrows?" Dryaka barked swinging his gaze to their captive.

"Let *me* ask her, Lord Dryaka," Elidor requested when the girl did not reply, seeing a way in which she might return to the High Priest's favour.

Dryaka looked from the woman to Dawn, glancing for a moment at her manacled wrists and then raising his eyes to her face. Finding no fear on the beautiful features, he said, "You'll find it less painful to answer me."

"Answer the Lord Dryaka!" Elidor commanded, and without giving Dawn an opportunity to do so she glided forward and drew back her left fist, "or you'll get more of this!"

With that, confident that she had little to fear from the girl, the woman shot her fist forward in a straight punch. It did not reach its intended mark, the centre of Dawn's face. Having read the other's intentions from her expression, the girl was ready to counter them.

Stepping back a short distance with her right foot

and turning it outwards, Dawn crossed her hobbled wrists and threw them up. While the fetters did not allow her to separate her hands, the connecting links gave her enough play to form a *karate* X-block. Intercepting Elidor's advancing arm, she forced it higher than it was supposed to go. Simultaneously, the girl brought her left foot around until it was almost touching the woman's left sandal. By bending her knees, Dawn lowered her body a little. Then, freeing her wrists from the block, she snapped around and propelled her left elbow into Elidor's midsection.

The woman might have counted herself fortunate that Dawn could not put her full power into the blow. Even at reduced force, it arrived hard enough to drive Elidor back a few steps and make her fold over. However, she did not go down. Nor was she badly hurt, as was shown by the way she lunged forward meaning to butt the girl in the chest.

Moving aside, Dawn avoided the attack and, pivoting, delivered a kick to Elidor's rump as she went by. Squawking in fury, the woman stumbled onwards and barely avoided sprawling on to her face. She retained her equilibrium with an effort, halted by the table and turned. With her beautiful features distorted by rage, she sent her right hand flying to the hilt of her sword.

Hearing the commotion, the two women who were preparing a meal in the kitchen portion of the pavilion ran in to investigate. Standing by the entrance, Dryaka waved for them to keep back. He was watching the fight with interest and enjoyment, so did not want it brought to an end by their intervention. He considered that it was a good test for the foreign girl and would give him an idea of how she might fare against Charole.

Darting in a curve towards Elidor, Dawn bounded into the air. Wrapping her legs around the woman's head, she allowed herself to hang down. When her shoulders came into contact with the silk covering of the pavilion's floor, she twisted herself away from her opponent. Bowed forward by the girl's weight, Elidor turned a half somersault and alighted on her back with the sword flying from her hand.

In performing the flying head-scissors, Dawn had failed to take into consideration that her hands would not be available to help her break the fall. So, while the throw was successful, the impact of her meeting with the floor had been more severe than she anticipated. By the time she had shaken off its effects, rolled on to her stomach and was starting to rise, Elidor had already come to her feet.

Ignoring her sword in her eagerness to retaliate for the punishment she had been taking, Elidor darted across the floor. While she was clenching her right hand ready to strike, her left fingers dug into Dawn's tawny hair and heaved. Squealing an involuntary protest at the pain being caused to her scalp, the girl reacted fast. As she was being dragged erect, she thrust both her fists upwards and into the base of the woman's imposing bosom. Although Dawn did not save herself entirely, her attack reduced the force with which Elidor's right cross connected against the side of her jaw. However, the left to her bust was harder and it was followed by a straight right to the face which sent her reeling backwards. Blood ran from the corner of her mouth, but she kept on her feet.

Going after Dawn, Elidor was taking a warning from her earlier attempts and knew that the other was anything but the easy meat which she had anticipated. Wanting to distract the girl from her true purpose, she swung up both hands as if she was meaning to plunge them into and pull her hair. Having done so, on coming into range, she whipped forward her right foot in a kick. To make sure of her aim, she glanced down.

It was a mistake!

Noticing Elidor's action, Dawn was not fooled. Taking a stride to the rear with her left foot and lowering her hips slightly, she drove her manacled wrists in a downwards swing that knocked the rising leg aside. Returning her foot to the floor, Elidor lashed a left hook at the girl's head. Forming the X-block again,

Dawn once more deflected the blow over her head. Spitting out a curse, Elidor fetched her right fist around in a hook aimed at the girl's stomach. Before it could land, Dawn had interposed her crossed wrists and halted it. Having done so, the girl twisted and flung her right elbow as hard as she could into Elidor's *solar plexus*.

Seeing the attack coming, Elidor tried to jump clear. The elbow landed, but was almost at the end of its flight. She grunted as it hit, then grabbed hold of Dawn's left wrist with her right hand. Jerking in an attempt to pull the girl off balance, Elidor struck her in the chest with the other fist.

Instead of trying to tear herself free, Dawn fought to hold her equilibrium. Achieving her purpose, she stepped forward with her left foot so that it pointed towards the outside of Elidor's advanced right leg. While she was doing so, she twisted sharply to her right so that her left elbow was exerting leverage against the woman's grasp. Dawn then took a short, swift step to the right with her right foot. Setting her weight on that leg, with its knee slightly bent, she leaned away from Elidor and stamped with her left heel against the other's forward knee. Pain caused Elidor to release her hold and retire a step. Pivoting before the woman had gone beyond her reach, Dawn flung a second stamping kick that took her in the pit of the stomach. It landed with all the driving thrust of the girl's gluteus muscles behind it.

Letting out a strangled gasp, Elidor folded over at the waist. Linking her fingers, Dawn swung them as if wielding a baseball bat. Her knuckles caught the side of the woman's head. Twirling around, Elidor crashed to and rolled over on the floor.

"Stop her!" Dryaka ordered, as Dawn went after her opponent.

Running forward, the two women grabbed the girl by the arms from behind. They were strong enough to restrain her. Nor did she struggle too hard, believing that the fight was over. However, having halted on her hands and knees, Elidor forced herself erect. For a moment, she stood swaying on spread apart feet. Then she stumbled forward with her hands crooked like talons.

Bracing herself against the two women's grasp, Dawn swung her legs from the floor. The soles of her bare feet lashed up to meet Elidor's jaw. Back snapped the woman's head and her charge turned into an even more rapid retreat. Twirling helplessly, she collapsed face foremost on the table which buckled under her weight. She made an involuntary attempt to rise, then slumped forward and lay still.

The women threw Dawn to the floor before she could return her feet to it. Already breathing hard from her exertions, the landing winded her and she flopped limply. However, before the women could do anything more to her, Dryaka barked an order for them to leave her alone.

"Go and attend to Elidor," the High Priest ordered. "Then bring water and food for the foreign girl."

Waiting until the women had taken Elidor by the arms and dragged her into the kitchen section of the pavilion, Dryaka turned his gaze to Dawn. She was already sitting up and he studied her with satisfaction. Despite the failure to obtain her bow and arrows, he felt sure that she would serve his original purpose. If she could defeat Elidor while her wrists were shackled together, she would have a good chance against Charole with her hands free. Except that the end would be different. When Dawn fought against the Protectress, it would be to the death.

CHAPTER FOURTEEN

You're Not A Mun-Gatah

The Protectress of the Quagga God was in anything but a pleasant mood as she rode alone across the plains about two miles from the Mun-Gatahs' hunting camp in the late afternoon.

Ever since Charole had watched—through a slit specially made in the wall of her pavilion tent's sleeping quarters—Elidor's party returning with the foreign girl as their prisoner, she had been filled with an ever-growing sense of annoyance and perturbation. Not even receiving the news that Dawn had defeated the High Priest's main female adherent in a fight despite having had her wrists secured by a pair of hobbles, made the Protectress feel any better.

On being told Mador's version of the hunt for the foreign girl, Charole had not been surprised to hear that her half-sister's party had separated from the other faction. So, although she was puzzled by Sabart and Chanak allowing their rivals to take the *grar-gatah* belonging to the dead eagle's attendant, she had no suspicion of foul play having been done nor did she fear that her supporters would not be coming back.

Just about the only consolation Charole was able to draw from the situation was in thinking of Dryaka's disappointment over his party's failure to bring the girl's bow and arrows with them. Although he had not referred to the weapons when sending the party after their owner, the Protectress had guessed that he wanted to lay his hands upon them.

Wanting to avoid having to put up with the High

Priest's smug satisfaction, Charole had anticipated his invitation to go and see the prisoner by taking her quagga and leaving the camp. She knew where to find a party of her supporters who were hunting and was heading for them. However, she was grateful for the opportunity to ride alone as it gave her time to think. She was aware of the threat to her position. After the failure of her eagle, and of Ragbuf and Sabart's party, the people might start to believe that she was no longer in the Quagga God's favour.

Something had to be done to restore her prestige, Charole told herself. The problem she must solve was what should she do? It would, she realized, have to be something important or spectacular to off-set her string of misfortunes and failures. Dryaka was building up too much superiority for anything of a trivial nature to bring her back level with him.

Thinking of the High Priest's recent successes brought up another matter upon which Charole had not been able to gain any enlightenment. She was very curious about the reason for him being called back to the camp the previous day. With his interest in the foreign girl and her weapons, only a matter of considerable importance would have made him leave the hunt for the girl in his adherents' hands. Although Charole was aware that his recall was connected with Zongaffa, that was the extent of her knowledge.

Despite all her efforts, Charole had not yet been able to find out what it was that the aged herbalist had discovered. All she could be sure of was that Dryaka regarded it as being of the greatest importance. However, she had recently been fortunate enough to have obtained the services of one of the High Priest's serving-women. So, even if she could not gain possession of the secret, she had hopes of solving the mystery that surrounded it.

Having become engrossed in her thoughts, Charole was almost oblivious of her surroundings and far less alert than usual. She was passing along the bottom of a valley and approaching a fairly sharp bend. The gentle slopes on either side were generously coated with large clumps of bushes, some of which effectively concealed what lay around the curve. All in all, it was not the kind of terrain through which she would normally have ridden in such an incautious fashion.

The folly of the Protectress's behaviour was brought home to her in no uncertain manner. If she had been less deeply involved in her thoughts, she would have heard and been warned by various sounds which were emanating from the valley beyond the bend.

Suddenly, when Charole was about a hundred yards from the curve, something huge and black came dashing from beyond it. Slammed out of her reverie, she realized that she was confronted by just about the worst kind of animal with which she could have come into contact under the circumstances.

The Protectress's quagga stallion was a good mount. Fast, agile, possessing stamina of a high order, under most conditions it was steady and completely trustworthy. However, there was one creature which terrified it and with good cause. During its training as a combined hunting and war-charger, it had been attacked by a bull buffalo. Although it had not been gored or even seriously injured, despite having been thrown, the fright which it had received had made it unreliable in the presence of such an animal.

Already being pursued by the party of hunters whom Charole was meaning to join, the enormous bull buffalo took the gravest exception to finding its path being blocked by yet another rider. Letting out a thunderous bellow, it tossed the great, fifty-eight-inch span of its massive curved horns and rushed onwards with the intention of removing the latest and closest of its human foes.

Unfortunately for Charole, the realization of her peril came just a moment too late.

Letting out a startled scream at the sight of what it regarded as being a mortal enemy, the previously well-behaved quagga displayed its antipathy. Its erstwhile leisurely walking gait changed abruptly into a rearing pivot and lunge away from the source of its terror.

Such was the violence of the quagga's panic-induced reaction and the change in its motions that Charole, taken completely unawares, was unable to counter them. Nor, excellent rider though she was, could she avert the disaster which befell her.

Slipping backwards as the quagga reared, the Protectress began to tighten her legs so that she would not slide over the cantle. While she succeeded, the turning movement tilted her to the right and as her mount started to run the propulsion of its hindquarters' powerful thrust dislodged her. Instinctively kicking her left leg free as she felt herself being thrown from the saddle, she found to her dismay that her right foot had become entangled with the stirrup iron. So, while she had just enough coordination to break some of the force with which she hit the ground, she could not prevent herself from being dragged along as her mount bolted. Nor, with the buffalo thundering after them, was there any likelihood of the quagga heeding the gasped out commands to stop that she was giving it.

From behind the clump of bushes, where he had halted and taken cover when Charole first came into view, Bunduki watched what was happening. Although—even dressed as he was—he had no wish to come into contact with a member of the Mun-Gatah nation, he realized that the woman was in deadly peril and needed help.

After having spent a restless, anxious and worrying night, the blond giant had set out to find his adoptive cousin as soon as day had broken. He had killed a bush-buck before parting from Joar-Fane and At-Vee, leaving them with sufficient meat to last until the hunter's ankle was healed. Promising that he would return if he was successful in his bid to locate and rescue Dawn, he had made preparations for the quest.

Having learned from At-Vee that the Mun-Gatahs lived on the open plains, along with such other details as the hunter could supply to augment the scanty information already given by Joar-Fane, Bunduki had appreciated the difficulties of tracking Dawn's captors without being seen. That would apply particularly as he intended to make use of the zebras which had belonged to Joar-Fane's late pursuers.

Returning to the clearing where the fight had taken place, the blond giant had removed the garments from the man whose back he had broken. He had known that his blond hair and lighter skin would give him away, so he had also donned his victim's sleeveless over-tunic with the rearing quagga insignia. According to At-Vee, members of the People-Taker's escorts always wore them. With its cowl drawn up, it would conceal his hair and face more effectively than one of the leather helmets. The corpse's greaves and sandals, although the former were a rather tight fit, had completed the disguise.

The next problem to be faced had been that of armament. When discussing his plan with the Telonga couple, Bunduki had reluctantly concluded that he could not take along his bow and arrows if he wanted his disguise to serve its purpose. The Mun-Gatahs never used such weapons. Even if they had, the bows would not have been like the blond giant's fiber glass Bear Super Kodiak. If the Mun-Gatah saw what appeared to be a member of their nation armed in such a fashion it would arouse interest, if not outright suspicion, which it was important that he should avoid.

Having given the matter some thought and talked it over with At-Vee, Bunduki had decided to restrict his weapons to the Smithsonian bowie knife and the spears that were hanging from the three zebras' saddles. He had examined one of them and felt sure he could use it effectively if the need arose. So he had left Dawn's and his bows with the two Telongas. As At-Vee had disclaimed all knowledge of archery, although some of his people's hunters practised it, the blond giant had unstrung both of the bows.

Setting off upstream in the direction from which At-Vee had heard Dawn give the distress call of a she-

Mangani, Bunduki had ridden one of the *ocha-gatahs* and led the other and the *banar-gatah*. That had been less difficult than he had anticipated as all of the animals were used to being handled in such a fashion. He had found Dawn's and her pursuers' tracks, following them to the clearing in which she had been captured. The patches of dried blood on the ground had been sufficiently disturbing for him to have investigated the bushes around and he had found the two bodies. Realizing that Dawn could not have inflicted the injuries, particularly as the corpses' zebras had been slaughtered in the hiding place, he had deduced what must have happened.

Following the signs left by Dawn and her captors, Bunduki had found the third of Charole's murdered supporters along with his dead *banar-gatah*. The discovery had increased the blond giant's deep concern for his adoptive cousin's welfare. Even without the stories told by the Telonga couple, he realized that the Mun-Gatahs were a ruthless race who had small regard for the sanctity of human life.

Pressing on at the best speed his acquired mounts could manage, Bunduki rode relay on the two *ocha-gatahs*. He was reserving the *banar-gatah,* which was superior in quality, to be used in case of an emergency.

Reading the tracks had been somewhat easier out on the plains and the blond giant was making good time. For all that, the party he was following had had such a lead, he had not caught even a distant glimpse of them. The tracks appeared to be heading towards some smoke which was rising a long way ahead, but he was disinclined to take the chance that it was their destination and he continued following the trail.

Like Dawn, Bunduki had been impressed by the vast quantity and variety of the wild life that he had seen. However, such was the urgency of the situation and the need to keep watch for human enemies that he had taken neither the interest nor the pleasure in the animals which would have been the case in less demanding circumstances.

Once Bunduki had crossed the river, after having made a detour to examine what the hyenas and vultures had left of the two dead *Mun-Gatah* scouts and the zebra near the chasm, he had ridden upstream to the ford. He had been almost certain that the party he was following were going to the source of the smoke. Exercising greater caution because of the proof that there were other people—most probably Mun-Gatahs—in the area, he avoided showing himself upon the sky-line without first having scanned the terrain. As far as possible he kept to ground which offered some kind of concealment.

Bunduki had been descending into the valley when he had seen Charole and he had taken cover behind a sizeable clump of bushes. Such had been the Protectress's preoccupation with her various problems that she had been unaware of the blond giant's presence. He had considered that was all too the good. While his disguise would have been satisfactory at a distance, it would not have stood up to an examination at close range. The chief danger, to his way of thinking, had been that her mount would catch his zebras' scent and warn her that he was there. However, before she had gone far enough beyond his position, the buffalo had made its appearance.

Seeing Charole thrown and dragged by the animal which he identified as a quagga, Bunduki did not hesitate before going to her assistance. Nor did he give any thought to various sounds that suggested he might be doing the very thing he had hoped to avoid, allow himself to be seen by members of the Mun-Gatah nation.

Despite his size, Bunduki was a light rider and capable of sitting his mount so as to take less out of it than would a smaller, but less skilled, person. However, he had pushed the two *ocha-gatahs* hard and, about a quarter of an hour earlier, he had finally transferred to the fresher and more powerful *banar-gatah*.

Releasing the *ocha-gatahs'* reins, the blond giant set his mount into motion. It responded eagerly, showing no concern over being guided after the charging buffalo. Urging it to go faster, he thought how he might rescue the woman.

Obviously the first priority was to deal with the buffalo.

How to do it was the problem.

Bunduki's mother had been the granddaughter of the legendary Texas cowhand and gun fighter Mark Counter, one of whose feats had been to wrestle with and break the neck of a longhorn bull with his bare hands. Bunduki knew that, although he had learned how to "bulldog" as his illustrious forebear had done, it would not serve his purpose on this occasion. The buffalo was bigger and bulkier than any domesticated bull. It would have tipped the scales at more than the longhorn's nine hundred and seventy-five pounds' weight.

Nor did the blond giant consider that riding alongside the buffalo and trying to stab it to death with the spear, even if he could draw the weapon while travelling at speed, offered an acceptable solution. Having had to shoot some of the Cape sub-species of *Syncerus Caffer Caffer*—to which the enormous bull appeared to belong—on occasion as part of the Amagasali Wild Life Reserve's population control programme, he knew just how hard they were to kill, even when he was armed with a modern, double-barrelled .600 rifle. Dropping the great beast using a spear, quickly enough to save the woman would be almost impossible.

There was, Bunduki concluded, only one way to handle the situation.

It would be neither easy, safe, nor secure!

As a present for his seventeeth birthday, the blond giant's adoptive parents had taken him for a vacation to a ranch that was owned by his maternal grandparents in the Big Bend country of Texas. While there, he had become the best of friends with his look-alike American cousin.

Although Bradford Counter's ambition had been to

follow his "Great-Grandpappy Mark's" example by becoming a peace officer instead of entering the family's very lucrative oil business, he was in addition to either of these professions, a skilled cowhand. He had taught Bunduki to perform many of the tasks required for such work, including a method of dealing with recalcitrant cattle. As a member of the *Bovidae* family, the buffalo might be said to come into that category.

The great beast was running fast in its eagerness to reach, trample on, or gore, the quagga and the woman fleeing before it. However, even carrying Bunduki, the *banar-gatah* was capable of travelling at a greater speed than the buffalo's thirty-five miles per hour.

Measuring the decreasing distance between himself and the buffalo with his eyes, the blond giant settled himself more firmly in the saddle. If he had had a catch-rope he would have used it to "take up the buffalo's toes," as he had been taught by his Cousin Brad. Lacking the necessary tool for that purpose, he was compelled to resort to an even more tricky, demanding and risky procedure.

Closing the gap at a racing gallop, Bunduki steered the still responsive *banar-gatah* at an angle that would take them to the right of the buffalo. Like all of its kind, the bull was running with its tail extended poker-stiff behind it and parallel to the ground. It was oblivious of the rapidly approaching pursuer.

Out stabbed the blond giant's left hand, to catch hold of the buffalo's tail. Having obtained his hold, he gave a sudden jerk with all his strength. Simultaneously, he let out a yell and kicked the *banar-gatah's* ribs with his heels. Receiving the signal, the gallant animal lunged forward with an increased velocity. Even so, the blond giant wondered if it could move fast enough to save both their lives.

Due to the speed that it was travelling the massive beast was thrown off balance, despite its two thousand pounds' weight. Its hind legs were snapped to the left and the fore limbs buckled. Turning heels over head, it alighted with a shattering crash that knocked every atom of air from its lungs.

For all the apparent ease with which Bunduki had brought the buffalo down, his task had been anything but simple. It had called for courage, skill and a well-trained mount of the finest quality.

However, the blond giant knew that his task was not yet at an end. The quagga was still racing along the valley, dragging its helpless burden behind it. Steering the *banar-gatah* in the required direction, Bunduki gave chase. Although he heard shouts from his rear, he did not look back.

Using all his skill, Bunduki acquired every bit of speed he could from the *banar-gatah*. Even so, he had to cover almost a hundred yards before he was drawing level with the woman's panic-stricken quagga. She was hanging limply, barely conscious after being dragged so far. For all that, she could count herself lucky. The short, but thickly growing grass was springy enough to have reduced the effect of the pounding.

Coming alongside the quagga from the left, so as to avoid the danger of his mount trampling upon the woman, Bunduki leaned across. The Mun-Gatahs used one piece reins, so they were hanging over the animal's neck instead of trailing down. Having made his catch, he straightened his legs and stood in the stirrups. Waiting until he felt that his mount's hind legs were coming under him and its balance was to the rear, he drew back on the reins.

"Whoa!" Bunduki yelled, sitting down and inclining his torso to the rear while thrusting his feet forward.

Obviously the Mun-Gatahs adopted a similar method when waiting to make a mount come to a halt quickly. Obediently the *banar-gatah* began to slide to a stop. Having no such control being exerted over it, the quagga ignored the command until the pull of its reins brought its head around. It swerved, tried to avoid the *banar-gatah* but failed to do so. They collided shoulder to shoulder and both went down.

Seeing that the collision was imminent and unavoidable, Bunduki snatched his feet from the stirrups and dived to the left. He landed rolling, as he had learned to do when being thrown by a horse, and regained his feet as quickly as he could.

Ignoring half a dozen male Mun-Gatahs who were galloping towards him, while four more plunged lances into the still recumbent buffalo, Bunduki ran behind the *banar-gatah* as it and the quagga were struggling to rise. When donning the dead warrior's garments, he had slit the tunic down its left side so as to allow him unimpeded access to his bowie knife. Drawing the weapon from its sheath, he bounded over the woman. As he halted, he bent and grabbed her ankle with his left hand. Then he slashed through the stirrup leather, liberating her as quickly as he could. There was need for haste. The quagga was almost on its feet and he doubted whether it would be in an amiable frame of mind when it stood up.

Releasing the woman's leg, the blond giant threw himself forward. Fast as he moved, it was not quite rapid enough. The quagga's hind hooves lashed towards him and one of them struck him a glancing blow on the right elbow. Glancing, maybe, but it was still hard enough to numb his arm momentarily and caused him to drop the knife. Carried forward by the momentum of his leap, he advanced a couple of long strides. When he had stopped himself, one look told him that he could neither retrieve the weapon nor return and mount the *banar-gatah* before the approaching riders arrived.

He felt some slight consolation when he noticed that none of the six had a lance, although each was armed with a sword. Nor were any of the newcomers wearing a leather breastplate.* The foremost of them were al-

---

*Only the distrust that existed between the High Priest and the Protectress had caused their hunting party to wear breastplates. They had pretended that their reason for doing so was the possibility of meeting enemies.

ready bringing their zebras to a stop and looking in the blond giant's direction.

Springing from his *banar-gatah's* saddle, the first man to arrive ran to where the woman was beginning to sit up and gaze dazedly about her. Her quagga had gone along the valley, bounding and kicking up its heels. Snapping an order over his shoulder as he knelt by Charole, the man sent one of the *grar-gatah* riders galloping after her mount. The rest of the party dismounted and, appaerntly having disposed of the buffalo, the others were approaching.

A burly *ocha-gatah* rider detached himself from the quartet who were on foot and slouched towards Bunduki. Glancing from the big blond to the knife, the man did a double take as he realized belatedly that there was something wrong.

"Hoy!" the man yelped, springing forward and reaching for his sword. "You're not a Mun-Gatah! Who——?"

The question went unfinished. Instead of answering, Bunduki thrust out his left fist. It caught the man just below the breast bone, halting and folding him onto the right hook that was the blond giant's follow-up attack. Lifted upright, the man went over on to his back.

Attracted by their companion's yell, all but the *banar-gatah* rider kneeling by Charole turned. Seeing their companion felled, the three of them rushed at Bunduki. Looking around, the kneeling man realized that the Protectress's rescuer was not a Mun-Gatah. Immediately he wanted to know where he had acquired his garments. What was more, in addition to any information the blond giant might possess, he would make a fine sacrifice for the Quagga God.

"Take him alive!" roared the *banar-gatah* rider, coming to his feet and going to help enforce his command.

That proved to be much easier said than done.

Hearing their leader and being aware of what would happen if they should go against his wishes, the men did not attempt to draw their swords. Instead, they fanned out and closed on Bunduki from three different points. Like the other warriors with whom he had fought, each of the trio wanted to gain the acclaim of capturing him. So they were acting as individuals rather than a team.

Swifter than his companions, the man coming from the blond giant's left was nearest and received first attention. Catching the forward driving right wrist with his left hand, Bunduki prevented it from reaching him and snapped a side kick into the man's ribs. Having done so, the big blond threw up his right hand to deflect the punch being thrown by the nearest warrior on that side and halted the advance of the other with a back kick to the body.

Although still shaken by her experience, Charole had recovered sufficiently to sit up and take notice. She saw Bunduki dealing with the first three attackers. Then, as the *banar-gatah* rider rushed up and the blond giant ducked under his grabbing hands. Catching the man around the knees, Bunduki straightened and pitched him head over heels.

Watched by the fascinated woman, the three men flung themselves *en masse* at the blond giant. They were, as she knew, trained warriors as good as any in the Mun-Gatah nation. Yet, for all their capability, they could not subdue the big stranger, even with the help of the *banar-gatah* rider.

It took the combined efforts of the entire hunting party to quell Bunduki. Nor did they succeed for a good fifteen minutes (as he measured time). Throughout it, he used every bit of skill and strength he possessed, calling upon the various unarmed combat techniques which he had acquired. By the end of the fight, three of the Mun-Gatahs were down with broken bones and a fourth lay dead, his neck snapped like a rotten twig.

Standing and looking down at the blond giant's mighty body, now bruised, bloody and stripped to only the leopardskin loincloth, Charole felt a sense of elation. At last, providing she could win him over, she was certain she had found a man who was capable of helping her to overthrow the High Priest.

CHAPTER FIFTEEN

I Alone Stand Between You And Death

"YOU fight very well, Dawn of the Apes," Dryaka remarked, entering the main section of his pavilion tent carrying the Randall Model 1 fighting knife in his right hand. "They tell me that Elidor's jaw is broken. She always did talk too much, so it might be an improvement."

Dawn Drummond-Clayton was puzzled and not a little perturbed as she watched the High Priest of the Mun-Gatah nation approaching. While the oil lamps which had been lit at sundown did nothing to soften the savage lines of his features, he seemed almost jovial and friendly.

After having defeated Elidor, the girl had expected to be beaten up by the two serving women, or put to torture if not killed. Instead, apart from having been kept manacled by the hobbles and under observation at all times to prevent her from trying to remove them, she had practically been treated like a guest.

On their return from attending to the unconscious Elidor, the women had carried out the High Priest's orders regarding the prisoner. They had bathed the dried blood from Dawn's face, allowed her to drink and had given her a good meal. From the way they had talked and acted, the girl had concluded that they were not entirely averse to the beating she had given to their superior.

Accepting that—watched as she was by the women and with male guards close by—there could be no hope of escape, Dawn had not attempted to do so. After the meal, she had made a bed from some of the pillows and rested on it. She had wanted to rebuild her strength in case an opportunity to get away should present itself, or to be ready if Elidor came back in search of revenge.

The rest of the afternoon had passed without incident. Despite the reason Dryaka had given to the Elders for having Dawn brought into his pavilion, he had not attempted to question her. In fact, he had left her in the care of his adherents and had gone off about some business of his own.

Night had fallen before the High Priest had returned. From the expression on his face as he stalked from the main entrance to his sleeping quarters, the girl concluded that whatever the business which had occupied him had been it had failed to come up to his expectations. However, apart from glancing at Dawn and asking the serving women if all was well, he had taken no notice of her. She estimated that over an hour had elapsed since she had last seen him.

"Bring food, then leave us," Dryaka ordered, without giving the girl an opportunity to answer his comment about Elidor.

"My father and his men will be coming to rescue me," Dawn stated, as the High Priest sat on the cushion which one of the serving women had placed in front of her. "You've seen how effective even a woman's bow and arrows can be. Many of your people will die if I'm harmed."

"Yes," Dryaka said, showing no perturbation over the warning. Instead, he looked pointedly at the knife in his hand and went on, "Your 'Suppliers' have given you excellent weapons. Far better than anything we've received. Where and how do they make their deliveries?"

"I don't know——," Dawn began, genuinely puzzled by the question.

"And you claim to be the daughter of the Apes' leader!" Dryaka ejaculated, before the girl could finish. "Don't trifle with me, or it will be the worse for you.

I alone stand between you and death. Charole wants your blood for killing her eagle. Only I can give you the chance of fighting for your life instead of being sacrificed to the Quagga God."

Dawn had been meaning to say that she did not know what the High Priest had meant by "Suppliers." She had hoped to obtain information about a matter which had been puzzling her.

After the girl had rested earlier in the day, having no desire to let her muscles become stiffened by inactivity, she had risen and started to walk around. Although she had not been permitted to leave, she had studied the camp from the pavilion's front and rear entrances. Then she had turned her attention to the interior of the tent.

Like Bunduki when he had been looking at the property of the dead Mun-Gatah warriors, Dawn was puzzled by what she saw. The materials from which the pavilion and its furnishings were made of a far higher and more sophisticated quality than she would have believed her captors were capable of producing. In fact, they had the feel and appearance of modern synthetic fabrics. The lamps, weapons and other metallic objects that she had examined also seemed to have been made by machines.

Apparently the Mun-Gatahs and, judging from the High Priest's question, the other primitive nations had some source of supply which was capable of manufacturing their requirements. Yet, even if such a technically advanced people had wanted to retain a monopoly on trading with the otherwise undiscovered races, it was unlikely that they would be able to keep their activities a secret.

Unless, of course, Dawn's theory regarding her whereabouts should be correct.

Fantastic and unbelievable as it seemed, the girl was growing even more certain that she had guessed the truth.

"Come now," Dryaka went on, interrupting Dawn's train of thought and adopting a more placatory attitude after having delivered the threat. He also dropped his voice and darted a glance at the kitchen portion of the pavilion, continuing, "I'm willing to tell you that our 'Suppliers' put them in the caves beneath the Quagga God's temple."

"I don't know where our 'Suppliers' make their deliveries," Dawn answered and, seeing anger darken her interrogator's face, knew that she would have to do better than that. Having noticed how he had behaved and spoken when giving her the information, she had an inspiration. "I'm Tarzan's *youngest* daughter. Only he and his oldest son and daughter are allowed to know the secret."

Being aware that the subject of the mysterious "Suppliers" was tabu amongst his own people and the other races with whom he had come into contact, Dryaka was willing to accept the girl's explanation. However, he was disappointed as he always was whenever he made an attempt to solve the mystery of the "Suppliers." He had hoped that the "Apes" might have different beliefs on the subject, or that Dawn—being the "daughter" of her nation's leader—had access to the required information.

"Where is your home?" the High Priest asked, raising his voice to its previous level as he left the potentially dangerous business of discussing the "Suppliers."

"On the edge of the jungle, far to the east," Dawn replied.

"What brought you to land of the Mun-Gatahs?" Dryaka inquired.

"I had often heard of your people," the girl lied, but so convincingly that she might have been speaking the truth. "So I thought I would come and see what you were really like. Then a lion frightened my mount——."

"Your people are riders?" Dryaka interrupted.

"We are," Dawn confirmed, and decided, in view of his surprise, that a little boasting might not come amiss. "But our mounts are bigger, and stronger and faster than anything I've seen here."

"It's *very* strange that I've never heard of you," Dryaka said, pensively and almost dubiously.

"Our land is very far away," the girl countered. "And we guard its borders jealously. We usually stay within them and kill any strangers who try to enter."

"I see," the High Priest grunted. On various occasions, Mun-Gatah raiding parties or individuals had disappeared without a trace. They could have fallen foul of the "Apes." That would explain why none had returned to brings news of a well-armed and dangerous nation. "How many of your people are there?"

"We have five large cities," Dawn told him, seeking a happy medium between failing to impress him with her "nation's" numbers, and arousing suspicion through over-exaggeration.

"*Five!*" Dryaka repeated, in a mixture of awe and disbelief. "No other nation has more than *one!*"

"We aren't like the other nations," Dawn pointed out with complete conviction and well simulated disdain.

From the brief flicker of emotion which crossed the High Priest's swarthy face, the girl guessed that her thrust had gone home. So it had. Dryaka dropped his gaze to the Randall knife and remembered the quality of her bow and arrows, realizing that all were far superior to anything that the Mun-Gatahs and other nations owned.

"I'm sorry for the way you were treated, Dawn," the High Priest declared, trying to look contrite and pleasant. "It was all the fault of those fools I sent to ask you to come and visit me in peace."

At that moment, preventing Dryaka from continuing with the lying apology, the flaps at the rear of the pavilion were opened. Looking about him in a nervous manner, a short, chubby man entered. He wore the undecorated attire of a *grar-gatah* rider, but did not have the appearance of being a warrior.

"I bring news, Lord Dryaka!" the newcomer announced hurriedly, throwing a glance towards the closed front entrance and speaking in a low voice.

Then his gaze swung to Dawn and he pointed at her. "Charole has brought in a prisoner. He is a very big man, dressed like a Telonga, but with skin like this woman's. His hair is white, but he isn't old and he is very muscular. The knife they took from him is almost as long as our swords and like no other I've ever seen."

Only by exercising all of her self control could Dawn hold her emotions in check. Even so, she failed to prevent herself giving a little gasp as the import of the man's information struck her. Unless she was mistaken, he had brought terrible news. The person whom he described sounded very much like her adoptive cousin.

If it was Bunduki, he too had fallen into the hands of the Mun-Gatahs!

Fortunately for the girl, her involuntary and brief response had gone unnoticed by the High Priest. He was scowling malevolently at the newcomer, a spy whom he had planted in the Protectress's retinue.

"I've heard nothing of this," Dryaka protested, for the arrival of a prisoner—particularly one as unusual as this man appeared to be—would normally have attracted sufficient attention to be reported to him. "When did it happen?"

"Soon after sundown," the spy replied and went on hurriedly in exculpation. "I haven't been able to get away until now, my lord. She had him brought to her pavilion secretly after it was dark. He is still there and she is treating him as well as—very well."

"Is she?" Dryaka growled, guessing that the man had intended to say, "as well as you are treating this girl," or words to that effect. "And you say that she's alone with him?"

"She was, my lord, but I couldn't hear what they were saying. I mustn't stay long, my lord, or I may be missed. There is something else I have to tell you."

"What is it?"

"Talgum and Altab came a few minutes ago, although she had said she was not to be disturbed. They brought a small bag which they said had come from your pavilion."

"A *small* bag?" Dryaka spat out and Dawn could see that he was deeply perturbed. "What was in it?"

"Only some black dust," the man answered in an off-hand fashion, meaning to go on by explaining that he would not have bothered to come and interrupt the High Priest except that Charole had appeared to be very excited over the contents of the bag.

There was, however, nothing off-hand about the way Dryaka responded on hearing the reply.

"The Thunder Powder!" the High Priest almost bellowed, springing to his feet and dropping the Randall knife. Without bothering to retrieve the weapon, he dashed towards his sleeping quarters, snarling, "If *she's* got any of it, I'll have somebody's life!"

* * * * * *

"And just what might *this* be?" demanded Charole, staring disdainfully at the small pile of black powder which the leader of the party who had captured Bunduki was pouring on to her pavilion's table.

"I don't know," Talgum answered, speaking thickly due to his badly swollen mouth. Stopping the flow, he placed the bag alongside the Smithsonian bowie knife on the table. For a moment, he stared enviously at the weapon. Then, darting a hate-filled scowl at its owner, he went on, "The woman said it was what Zongaffa was making for Dryaka."

Lounging on the cushions which the Protectress had placed near the table for him, with his wrists linked together by a set of hobbles, but otherwise unfettered, Bunduki studied the powder. He thought he recognized it. If he had, it might enable him to escape.

On recovering consciousness, the blond giant had been surprised to find that he had not received any more serious injuries than the various bruises and abrasions gathered during the fighting. He had soon discovered that he owed his salvation to the influence of the beautiful, sensual, if dishevelled woman whose life he had saved. For all that, he had sensed there was more than gratitude behind her protection.

Although Bunduki had been taken to a nearby stream where his injuries were given the same treatment as the warriors who had suffered at his hands, Charole had insisted that they should delay rejoining their companions until after night had fallen.

While they were waiting, Charole and Talgum had questioned Bunduki about how he had come into possession of the Mun-Gatah garments and zebras. Knowing that to refuse supplying the information could have painful consequences, he had invented a story of how he had been attacked by, and had killed, three members of the People-Taker's escort. Having identified the animals as belonging to some of the High Priest's adherents, his interrogators had seemed more pleased than angry at what he had told them.

The blond giant had discovered, by listening to his captors, that his adoptive cousin was already a prisoner of the Mun-Gatahs. From what had been said, he had deduced that he was to be taken to the camp in which she was being held. It had been that, even more than a realization of the futility of trying to fight his way to freedom which had caused him to put aside the notion of attempting to escape while he was still in the hands of such a small party. He had wanted to be in a position where he might be able to help Dawn before doing anything that would cause his captors to increase the simple bonds of restraint which secured him.

From the way Bunduki's captors had behaved as they were bringing him into their camp, he had deduced that they wished to keep his presence a secret. On coming into sight of their companions' zebras, which were grazing and resting at liberty but under the eyes of guards, the *banar-gatah* rider—although as yet the blond giant had not learned the Mun-Gatahs' social distinctions—had gone ahead. Returning, he had warned that some of the High Priest's adherents were on duty watching over the herd. At the Protectress's orders, Bunduki had been made to dismount. Escorted by Talgum and two of the *ocha-gatah* riders, he had been taken to the camp on foot by a route which had kept them out of sight of the guards.

Once Charole had the blond giant safely delivered to her pavilion, she had left him in Talgum's charge while she made her preparations for trying to win him over. Bathing in the sleeping portion of her pavilion, she had rejoined the men clad in a very daring, diaphanous white gown. The way in which it had clung to the magnificent contours of her gorgeous body had shown that it and the high heeled pumps which had replaced her sandals were her sole garments.

Over a meal, with a scowling and obviously jealous Talgum as the other guest, the Protectress had tried to learn what had brought Bunduki to the Mun-Gatah country. On being questioned about other members of his nation, he had been careful not to reveal his true purpose. Charole had tried to find out if he was searching for Dawn, but his replies had left her convinced that he was not.

Dismissing the *banar-gatah* rider at the end of the meal, the Protectress had produced Bunduki's Smithsonian bowie knife. Like Dryaka was doing with Dawn, she had tried to elicit information regarding the means by which such exceptional weapons had been procured. Unconsciously, Bunduki had adopted a similar line to Dawn when explaining why he could not give details about their "Suppliers." He had also left his questioner with a profound impression of the strength, sagacity and numbers of the "Apes" nation.

Having decided that such efficient and capable warriors would make very useful allies, and believing that her captive was a very important leader of the "Apes," Charole had been even more determined to gain his support. She had used all her wiles and the full sensual attraction of her voluptuous body to achieve her ends. Applying the same kind of love-making techniques to which Bunduki was accustomed, she had been much more successful than Joar-Fane at learning his potential in that line.

Accepting that he might be able to use the woman of a means of attaining freedom for Dawn and himself, Bunduki had yielded to her seduction. The male Counters had always been noted for their lusty and prodigious prowess as makers of love and he had inherited the quality in full measure. So, even though his wrists were held by the hobbles, he had contrived to satisfy Charole's passions in a way that no other man had come close to doing.

Unfortunately, there had been an interruption before the blond giant could persuade the panting and submissive Charole to remove his bonds on the grounds that he would be able to do even better. Entering and apparently taking no notice of the sight of her mistress sprawling all but naked on the floor alongside the prisoner, one of the serving women had said that Talgum was outside and wished to speak with the Protectress. At first, Charole had been on the point of telling her maid to say she must wait. However, on learning that he was accompanied by the woman who was spying on Dryaka, the Protectress had changed her mind.

By the time Talgum had been granted permission to enter, in addition to replacing the blond giant's loincloth, Charole had dressed herself and tidied up her appearance. For all that, it had been clear the *banar-gatah* rider was aware of what had passed between them and disapproved of it.

"What do you think you're doing?" Talgum demanded suspiciously, reaching for his sword as Bunduki knelt up and bent his torso towards the table.

Apparently ignoring the question, but keeping his eye on the warrior, the blond giant held his hands out on the side furthest from the great bowie knife. Keeping them there, he leaned closer to the small pile of gritty black powder and sniffed at it. Despite the heavy aroma of Charole's perfume, a familiar smell came to his nostrils.

Taking her eyes from Bunduki at the evidence of his

good intentions, Charole gave a sharp and prohibitive shake of her head to Talgum. In the course of her successful seduction, she had talked of her desire to form an alliance with the blond giant and he had appeared to be fully favourable to it. She did not want anything to happen that might antagonize him against her and cause him to change his mind. So she kept her eyes on the warrior until, showing his annoyance, he thrust the half drawn sword back into its sheath.

"What are you doing, Bunduki?" Charole inquired, returning her gaze to the blond giant after having enforced her will on her supporter. "Do you know what it is?"

"I'm not sure," Bunduki answered, keeping his voice flat and emotionless. He hardly dared hope that his nose was not playing a trick upon him. Taking an even closer sniff, he felt a tingle of excitement as once again the odour of saltpetre mixed with sulphur and charcoal reached his ofactory organ. Still employing an even, almost disinterested tone, he straightened up and went on, "But I think I might."

"What is it?" the Protectress asked, hardly able to conceal her eagerness.

"I can't be certain," the blond giant admitted. "Can I touch it without your man cutting my hand off?"

"You can," Charole authorized, throwing another glare at Talgum.

Having been granted permission, Bunduki raised his hands. He wet the tip of his right forefinger and touched it lightly on the heap of powder. Tasting the grains which had adhered to it, he knew that he was correct. Seething with excitement, he made a wry face and spat. Then he rubbed his tongue vigorously on the back of his left hand.

"What *is* it?" Charole repeated and even Talgum looked impressed by the vehemence of the blond giant's reaction.

"I think it could be a deadly poison that the witch doctors of my people use," Bunduki answered and could see that his audience understood his meaning.

"There's one way to make certain. Put a lamp on the table."

"Why?" Talgum challenged, but Charole was already going to obey.

"What do you want it for, Bunduki?" the Protectress inquired, having taken down a lamp and set it on the table.

"To test the powder," the blond giant replied and reached for the bag.

"Here!" Talgum growled, stepping forward. "I'll do it."

"Go ahead," Bunduki sneered, knowing that such an attitude would probably bring about the result he required. "If you know what to do."

"Tell me and I'll do it," the warrior suggested, snatching up the bag as the big blond had expected he would.

"Tip the powder over the flame," Bunduki instructed and, when Talgum hesitated, went on in a mocking voice, "Let me do it, if you're afraid."

Giving an angry snort, the warrior up-ended the bag and a stream of black powder flooded from its mouth to fall towards the naked flame of the lamp.

CHAPTER SIXTEEN

Aaaah—Eeee—Aaaah—Eee—Aaagh!

LONG before the birth of Christ philosophers in Cathay—as China was then known—had learned that most spectacular and entertaining results could be produced from a mixture comprised of 41.2% saltpetre and 29.4% each of charcoal and sulphur.*

Although Zongaffa had never heard of Cathay, China, its philosophers, or Roger Bacon, *q.v.*, he had in some way contrived to dulpicate their discovery. However, like them, the aged Mun-Gatah herbalist had failed to appreciate the full potential of the resultant powder.

Having identified the "black dust" for what it was, Bunduki had been fully aware of its properties. Guessin that the other occupants of the pavilion tent were less well informed, he had paved the way for turning his superior knowledge to his and, he hoped, his adoptive cousin's advantage.

In addition to stepping away and allowing Talgum to start pouring the black powder from the cloth bag, the blond giant turned with his back to the table and closed his eyes. Being aware that breathing the atmosphere was going to be unpleasant in a short time, he also

*The figures quoted are actually those of the formula which was described by English philosopher, scientist and educational reformer, Roger Bacon, c. 1220–1292. There were many other prescriptions, including 76.64% saltpetre, 13.51% charcoal, 11.85% sulphur which would produce an ideal reaction and what came to be the universally standardized mixture, KNO_3–75%, C–15% and S–10%.

filled his lungs with air. So as to be ready if his plan should succeed, he pressed his elbows against his ribs and bent his forearms parallel to the well-padded floor of the pavilion.

Already suspicious of Bunduki's motives, Talgum noticed how he was acting. Suddenly, the *banar-gatah* rider sensed that he might be falling into a trap. Perhaps what he was doing could be very dangerous.

The realization came just a split-second too late!

Even as Talgum tried to stop the flow of powder, the first of the trickling grains reached the burning wick of the lamp. In the light of what happened, he could consider himself fortunate that the bag he was holding was not made of something stronger than cloth.

Bringing dry gunpowder into contact with a naked flame causes one of two results. If the grains are confined in a container which is capable of putting up resistance against the tremendous volume of gasses created by their ignition, there is an explosion. When the powder is weakly enclosed, or unconfined, the effects are less violent—but equally spectacular.

A spurt of fire leapt upwards from the lamp!

With a "whoosh!" sound, the bag erupted into flames and a billowing, rapidly increasing cloud of white gas!

Instantly, all was pandemonium inside the pavilion!

Engulfed by the full volume of the inferno, Talgum reeled backwards, his tunic alight. Almost choked by the swirling fumes, he could not scream despite the agony that he was suffering. Coughing in his attempts to do so, he twirled around. Going in the direction of the main entrance, he collapsed to roll over and over in the frenzy of his torment. His burning garments caused the silk-like padded covering on the floor to ignite. Once started, the flames spread across the inflammable material and reached, then began to consume, the front wall.

Being confident that she had won Bunduki over, Charole had not suspected that he was trying to trick her. However, seeing him turning his back, she sensed that the experiment could prove dangerous. So, without attempting to stop the warrior, she had started to back away. She was just far enough from the *banargatah* rider to avoid being caught in the blaze when the bag ignited. Startled by the effect, she let out a shriek which ended in a burst of coughing as the gasses created by the burning powder reached her. Throwing herself involuntarily to the rear, she tripped over a cushion and toppled backwards.

Without needing to turn, as he heard the sound of the detonation and felt the rush of heat strike his back, the blond giant put the rest of his scheme into operation. Bracing himself for the effort, he jerked his wrists apart. Such was the power exerted by his mighty muscles that the swivel link of the hobbles snapped as if it had been made of thin thread instead of metal.

Attracted by the commotion, Charole's maid and Talgum's companion dashed in from the kitchen portion of the pavilion. Letting out a screech of terror at what she saw, the woman rapidly retreated. Being made of sterner stuff, the man started to draw his sword and run towards Bunduki. Despite his courage, he was startled and not a little alarmed at the ease with which the blond giant broke free from the hobbles' confinement.

Having liberated his wrists, Bunduki sprang to the table. He saw the warrior approaching as his right hand closed on the hilt of the Smithsonian bowie knife. Scooping up the lamp with his left hand, he flung it at the man. Then, grasping the knife, he bounded over the table to the rear wall.

Glancing to his right, the blond giant saw the warrior deflect the lamp by knocking it aside with his left hand. It crashed to the floor by the rear wall and shattered. Gushing out, the fuel burst into flames and started a second blaze.

Swinging his right arm up and around in a forward circle, Bunduki sank the blade of his knife into the wall with a chopping motion. He could hear shouts of alarm being raised from various points, warning him that the disturbance and fire were attracting attention. By thrusting his left leg outwards and bending his right knee, he crouched and drew the knife downwards. Its edge sliced through the material without any difficulty.

However, even as the blond giant was cutting his way out, Talgum's companion was rushing closer and raising the sword ready to strike. Outside, the guards at each end of the pavilion saw what was happening. Grasping their lances, although they were on foot, they converged upon the opening that Bunduki's knife was making.

* * * * * *

Watching Dryaka rushing across the pavilion tent and into his sleeping accommodation, Dawn Drummond-Clayton wondered what he had meant by his cryptic reference to the "Thunder Powder." She could tell that he attributed a considerable amount of importance to it, whatever it might be. So much so that he had not noticed that he had dropped the Randall Model 1 fighting knife almost at her feet. What was more, his behaviour was causing the other occupant of the main portion to ignore her. The man who had brought the news was staring after the High Priest with his mouth hanging open was clearly oblivious of everything else.

Dawn was alert for any chance that might arise for her to escape. As yet, however, she could not see how she might turn Dryaka's perturbation to any great advantage. At best, it offered her the opportunity to arm herself. Reaching forward, keeping the spy and the flap through which the High Priest had passed under observation, she closed her hands around the hilt of the knife. It was her intention to hide the weapon under the cushion upon which she was sitting. If she was luck it would not be missed until the time came for her to make use of it.

Seeing Dryaka returning, Dawn knew she would not be able to carry out her plan before he saw her. So she turned the knife, hiding its hilt with her hands and, pushing aside the hobbles' connecting link, concealed the blade with her forearms. Studying the cold anger on his face, she decided he was so concerned by whatever he had discovered that he might not notice her weapon was missing.

While Zongaffa had not seen any practical application for the "Thunder Powder," Dryaka had sensed that it might be put to military use. The problem had been to find a way of utilizing it. Having sworn the old man to secrecy and prevented anybody else, even the Council of Elders, from learning of the experiments, Dryaka had been seeking some means of controlling the explosive qualities of the powder. He had been asked to return the previous day because the herbalist had believed they were approaching a break-through. For various reasons they had not been able to put the idea to the test so far. Their attempts to do so that afternoon had been frustrated, which had been the cause of his annoyance when he arrived in the pavilion that evening.

Due to his belief that the "Thunder Powder" would give him sufficient power to overthrow the Council of Elders and let him assume sole control of the Mun-Gatah nation, Dryaka wanted to keep all knowledge of its purpose and qualities to himself. Finding that one small bag was missing was cause for alarm and anger.

"Who took it?" the High Priest snarled, glaring at the spy.

"I—I d—don't kn—know," the man quavered, showing his fright at having to deliver a negative reply. "Talgum and——."

At that moment there was a dull "whoosh!" from somewhere beyond the front wall of the pavilion. An angry exclamation burst from the High Priest as he swung to stare in the direction from which the sound had originated.

For a moment, Dawn wondered if her ears were playing tricks on her. As a child, she had helped Bunduki experiment with the effects of igniting a pile of gunpowder. The noise it had made was almost identical to that which she had just heard. Then, as shouts rang out from different parts of the camp, she realized what the "Thunder Powder" must be.

Letting out a bellow of rage, Dryaka charged to and threw open the front entrance. As he was going out, Dawn saw the red glow of a fire growing rapidly bigger from the opposite pavilion. She knew that it was the one occupied by Charole.

Bunduki's captor!

Following his master's, example, the spy dashed out of the pavilion without giving Dawn a single thought. Coming to her feet, she changed the knife around so that its blade would be available for use. While she was doing so her eyes darted around. She guessed that Bunduki had contrived to set off the gunpowder as a distraction to help him escape. Judging from the commotion outside, he was having considerable success and she wanted to find some way of adding to the confusion.

Dawn's gaze went to the peak of the pavilion where a chandelier-like cluster of lamps was hanging. The cord by which it could be raised or lowered slanted down and was tied to one of the supports of the partition from the kitchen section.

Even as Dawn started towards the lower end of the cord, the serving women came from the kitchen one behind the other. Seeing the girl was not only standing, but was holding the knife, the leading woman stopped and opened her mouth to scream for help. Darting forward, Dawn bounded into the air to perform a drop-kick. Caught in the bosom by the girl's feet, agony numbed the woman's mind and chopped off her words before they could be spoken. What was more, the impact flung her backwards to collide with and knock over her companion.

Rebounding from delivering the attack, Dawn landed on her feet. Two strides took her to the cord. Grasping the knife's hilt in both hands, she cut through the strands. Down plunged the chandelier. On striking the floor, the four lamps burst and flames began to lick hungrily around.

Satisfied with what she had done, the girl ran to the

rear wall. Plunging in the knife, she slit open a gash long enough to form an exit. A glance through it told her that the sentries who had been at the rear were no longer there. Deciding that they must have gone to investigate the cause of the other disturbance, she stepped outside. Before she had taken more than half a dozen strides, she heard a yell from behind and to the left. A quick look that way warned her that at least one of them had heard the chandelier fall and was returning. There was a second yell, from the other side.

Without bothering to look, Dawn started to run through the darkness and the two sentries took up the pursuit.

* * * * * *

With the approaching warrior's sword lashing around at him, Bunduki dropped to the floor. Taken by surprise and missing his mark, the man's impetus carried him onwards. He tripped over the blond giant's legs and plunged headlong through the gap in the wall.

Seeing the warrior half in and half out of the tent, the guards did not wait to make an identification. Raising their lances as he sprawled face down, they drove the weapons to impale him before either realized he was making a mistake.

Leaping to his feet, Bunduki looked around him. The two fires were raging with unabated fury. However, Charole was already sitting up. Satisfied that she would be able to escape, he sprang through the gap. His appearance took the guards by surprise. Their weapons were still embedded in the warrior's body.

Noticing the guards were wearing metal helmets and breastplates, the blond giant based his strategy accordingly. Hurdling the body so that he passed between them, he struck at both simultaneously. In one respect, the man on the left fared somewhat better than his companion. He received the heel of Bunduki's clenched fist in the centre of the face, while the other guard was struck by the scalloped brass butt cap of the bowie's hilt. It was a small mercy, something like feeling grateful that one had been kicked by a horse instead of a mule. Each recipient was flung backwards with blood gushing from his smashed nostrils and mouth. Going down, neither of them was in any condition to interfere with the blond giant's departure.

Having made good his own escape, Bunduki's next concern was to rescue Dawn. He knew that she was being held in the High Priest's pavilion, or had been. There was a possibility that she had been moved elsewhere. With the whole camp aroused by the fire, searching for and reaching her would be difficult. Unless he could create another diversion, it might even endanger her life.

Hearing the snorting of the disturbed zebras not far away, Bunduki remembered something which his short acquaintance with them had taught him. An idea sprang to his head. Knife in hand, he loped swiftly towards the herd. Alert for any evidence that he was being pursued and hearing none, he selected a route which would keep him hidden from the animals' attendants. Keeping going until they were between him and the camp, he came to a halt. He noticed that a second fire was burning near the one that he had started. From its position, he guessed correctly that it was at the High Priest's pavilion.

Worried in case Dawn should be trapped in the second blaze, although he was also hoping that she might have caused it as an aid to escaping, the blond giant tossed back his head and cupped his hands about his mouth.

"Aaaah—eeee—aaaah—eee—aaagh!"

Deep, awesome and threatening, the challenge roar of a bull-*Mangani* thundered into the air!

The result was everything Bunduki had hoped to achieve!

Already made restless by the commotion at the camp, the zebras were milling in a worried manner. Startled by the menacing roar from so close at hand, they had one idea in their heads. To get away from whatever had caused the sound. That applied equally to the animals being used by the men who were guarding the herd. Rearing and plunging in terror, the majority of them threw their riders. Those which did not, bolted before the herd-guards on them could do anything to avert the panic. Within seconds of the call having been made, all of the zebras were stampeding recklessly towards the camp.

Having achieved his purpose, Bunduki set off after the animals, but at an angle which would take him to the rear of the second blazing pavilion.

Despite being encumbered by having her wrists manacled and the knife in her right hand, Dawn contrived to draw ahead of the two guards who were chasing her. They were carrying their long lances and had less inducement to speed. When the challenge roar thundered out, the girl felt her heart give a bound. There was no doubt in her mind as to who had made it. From behind her came startled exclamations as the pursuing Mun-Gatahs heard the call. Ahead, there were snorts of alarm, mingled with furious yells as men were thrown from their mounts. Then hooves drummed as the mass of zebras took flight.

Taking a chance of expanding much needed air from her lungs, Dawn answered Bunduki with the distress call of a she-*Mangani*. Once again, the pair of guards expressed their astonishment. Hoping to add to their consternation, the girl stopped to confront them.

Crouching slightly, grasping the knife with grim determination, Dawn peered through the surrounding gloom. As soon as she saw the two vague shapes starting to form, she repeated the call. From not too far away, although the sound of his running feet was being drowned by the rumbling caused by the stampeding zebras, Bunduki gave his reply.

Staring ahead of them, the two Mun-Gatahs could make out Dawn's figure. The faint light thrown by the stars did not permit great clarity of vision, but tended to distort it. To their eyes, the ill-seen form appeared to be very different from that of the beautiful and shapely girl who had emerged from the tent. That impression was increased by the sound which came from her.

Nor did the response which it received do anything to steady their nerves.

Brave enough under normal circumstances, the eerie sounds—associated with the mysterious and dreaded "Hairy People"—filled the two warriors with superstitious dread. Then they made out an even larger form that came looming out of the blackness. It proved to be the final straw. Discarding their lances, the pair spun around and fled toward the camp.

Dropping the knife as her pursuers ran away, Dawn turned. A moment later, she was in Bunduki's arms.

"Dawn!" the blond giant said. "Are you all right?"

"Yes," the girl confirmed. "Are you?"

"I am," Bunduki replied and a harder note crept into his voice. "Did any of them—?"

"No," Dawn assured him, knowing what the question had implied.

Releasing his adoptive cousin after having satisfied himself that she had not been harmed or sexually assaulted, Bunduki looked at the camp. Following the direction of his gaze, Dawn watched and listened to the confusion and pandemonium as the zebras rushed through it. Tents were collapsing and their erstwhile occupants were being scattered by the panic-stricken animals.

"We'd better get going," Bunduki suggested, after a few seconds. "I don't think they'll be coming after us just yet, but we might as well build up as good a lead as we can before they do."

"Can you get these hobbles off first, please?" Dawn inquired, holding out her hands. "Then I'll find my knife and we'll be going. It looks as if you've lost your bow and arrows, if you had them with you."

"I didn't," the blond giant answered, starting to unbuckle the hobbles. While he was setting the girl free and she was retrieving her knife, he explained why he had not been in possession of the weapons.

After a final check that nobody from the disrupted and ruined camp was coming, Dawn and Bunduki set off. Using the stars as a way of guiding themselves, they made for the ford across the river. It was their intention to rejoin Joar-Fane and At-Vee. Not only would they have a better chance of evading any pursuers from the plains-dwelling Mun-Gatah nation in the jungle, but they would be in possession of weapons with which to defend themselves and the two Telongas.

Knowing the need to keep constantly alert against the possibility of meeting dangerous animals, or so that they could detect any attempt that might be made to recapture them, Dawn and Bunduki kept as quiet as possible while walking along. Much as they would have liked to discuss the matter which was of such interest and importance to them both, they agreed to put it off until a more suitable occasion.

Daybreak found the girl and the blond giant at the edge of the river. They had reached it without incident, or hearing anything to suggest that the Mun-Gatahs were following them. Nor did they anticipate any difficulty in making the crossing. Wading into the ford side by side, they started to go over. As they were approaching the opposite bank, they saw something which brought them to a halt and sent their hands to the hilts of their knives.

Coming from nowhere, or so it seemed, something started to glow about ten feet from the river's edge. Faintly at first, it became brighter and brighter.

Neither Dawn nor Bunduki had ever seen anything like it in all their lives.

CHAPTER SEVENTEEN

Will You Go Back, Or Stay Here?

DAWN DRUMMOND-CLAYTON and Bunduki stared at the shimmering, intangible glow and wondered what it might be. They were not kept waiting long for an answer, but when it came neither of them was much the wiser. After a few seconds, the glow began to take shape as a tall, white-haired and venerable-looking old man clad in long, flowing white robes.

"Good morning, Miss Drummond-Clayton, Mr. Gunn," the figure said, in a gentle and pleasant voice. "Or may I call you 'Bunduki,' sir?"

"What the—!" the blond giant began.

"Please come out of the water," requested the man, or whatever it was. "There's no cause for you to be alarmed and your knives won't be needed."

"What shall we do, Bunduki?" Dawn inquired, glancing at her adoptive cousin in perplexity.

"Get out of the water," the blond giant answered, without taking his eyes from the figure. "Who are you?"

"You can call me your 'Supplier,'" the figure replied, still in friendly tones. "I should explain that this is not my real form. It is merely an appearance for your convenience, a conventionalization which allows you to see and communicate with us."

"But what are you?" Dawn insisted as she and Bunduki waded from the river.

"An alien life form so complex that you could not understand it," the "Supplier" answered.

"Then it must have been you who saved us when

199

the Land Rover went over the edge of the Gambuti Gorge," Bunduki guessed.

"It was," the "Supplier" confirmed. "And, as you both surmised, transported you to the planet you may call Zillikian. You have never heard of it. It lies exactly opposite Earth and follows the same orbit around the sun."

"If you were so close," Dawn said indignantly, "why didn't you stop whoever it was shooting M'Bili?"

"We are not permitted to interfere in such matters."

"You saved *us*," Bunduki pointed out.

"Only because there was no way in which you could have saved yourselves. I think it would be advisable for me to give you a full explanation."

"Can we walk while we're talking?" Bunduki requested. "If you're the one who's been watching me, you'll know that we didn't exactly leave the Mun-Gatahs in a peaceful and friendly manner."

"We have been keeping both of you under observation," the "Supplier" admitted, turning and starting to stride along between the girl and the blond giant with the vigour of a young man despite his aged appearance. "It is strange, but none of the others have ever been aware of our scrutiny. However, throughout your ages, we "Suppliers" have brought many life forms to Zillikian, including humanoids from Earth and other planets.

"The Telongas were the first human beings, brought from the South Sea island which had always been their home just before it was destroyed by a volcanic eruption. We settled them in villages in the jungle and began to supply their needs. As you have noticed, there are no noxious, nor disease-bearing insects here. Nor did the specimens—if you will excuse me referring to human beings in such a fashion—bring harmful germs and bacteria with them. During the transportation, we purged all such from their bodies to ensure that they would have nothing to prevent them from establishing their species.

"Incidentally, the reason you both felt so hungry on

recovering was that we subjected you to the same treatment, which includes emptying out your stomachs and alimentary tracts.

"But I digress.

"The Telongas established themselves in a way which exceeded our expectations. Given adequate protection against the predatory beasts, with their needs supplied by us and the jungle, their numbers increased at a truly amazing rate. Normally that could not have happened, as illness, starvation or warfare would have held the population in check.

"As the animals could not do it, we had to find some other means of control. So we decided that human predators were the only solution. The other nations of this continent maintain their own balances by raiding and fighting with each other, but none of them had come across the Telongas——."

"So you gave the Mun-Gatahs a similar kind of subconscious auto-suggestion, as you did Dawn and I, letting them know about the Telongas," Bunduki interrupted. "Was the People-Taker your idea too?"

"It was," the "Supplier" admitted. "That was to prevent them from de-populating the Telongas, who had been living in such ease that the majority of them had lost all will, or knowledge, of how to defend themselves against human foes. The People-Taker removes only sufficient of the population to maintain a natural balance. In return, the Mun-Gatahs protect the Telongas against the other nations."

"And you supply them all with arms, clothing, equipment, most of their needs, in fact," Dawn guessed.

"We do. Each nation has its supply point, to which we deliver their needs."

"And that means they never need to invent anything, or to advance technically," Bunduki stated.

"Is that such a bad thing?" the "Supplier" challenged mildly. "You have seen what technical advancement has done to Earth."

"You could have a point there, sir," the blond giant conceded. "Your supplying them accounts for why their

property looks as though it has been made by more sophisticated machines than they seemed capable of in-
venting. But why did you rescue Dawn and I and fetch
us here?"

"It has long been our wish to do so with a pair from
your family," the "Supplier" replied. "But we are not
permitted to remove any life form from its natural
habitat unless it is on the point of dying. Every time we
saw one of your family in danger, we computed that,
no matter how serious the situation might be, they
would contrive to escape. There was no way that you
could have survived. So we collected you and equipped
you for your presence here. Your facility for learning
languages was of the greatest use, allowing us to give
you the means to communicate with members of any
nation with whom you come into contact. For the
rest, post-hypnotic suggestion informed both of you that
the other was alive and gave you rough directions where
to find each other. You might call it an initiative test
and, I may say, you have passed it with great success."

"Do you mean that you manipulated the meetings
we had with the *Mangani* and all the others?" Bunduki
demanded angrily.

"No," the "Supplier" assured the blond giant. "That
was pure chance."

"I'd still like to know why you brought us here,"
Dawn insisted and Bunduki nodded his agreement.

"To offer you much the same position as you held in
Ambagasali, Bunduki," the "Supplier" explained. "We
want you to be the Chief Warden of Zillikian."

"Have I any choice?" asked the blond giant.

"We can take you back to Earth, but you will have
difficulty in explaining how you came to escape from
the Land Rover. I'm afraid that time travel, at least
as far as going back through it, is still only feasible in
the works of your science-fiction writers and a week has
elapsed since the incident."

"Then our people will have heard and think we're
dead," Dawn gasped.

"We have already informed them that you are alive,"

the "Supplier" said calmly. "Lord Greystoke says that he leaves the decision to you. Will you go back, or stay here?"

As the "Supplier" dropped back a couple of steps, Dawn and Bunduki looked at each other. It did not occur to them that he might have been lying, even with regard to his having notified their families of what had happened to them. Any nation, or culture, capable of doing what he had claimed and clearly could do, would have no difficulty in communicating with the Greystokes even though they were living in Pellucidar at the Earth's core.

Much the same thoughts were running through Dawn's and Bunduki's minds.

Should they accept the offer and remain on Zillikian?

Except for the absence of the other members of their family, the planet offered everything that the girl and the blond giant had so often discussed and wished that they could find. It was primitive, brutal perhaps, violent certainly; but completely natural, unspoiled, free from the mental and physical pollution of Earth and its bitter social conflicts.

To Bunduki, the prospect of staying was intriguing. He would be in much the same position of Chief Warden as he had been in the Ambagasali Wild Life Reserve. Yet here the task would be so much more complex and interesting. It would be a challenge and he could never resist a challenge.

Watching her adoptive cousin, although she was already starting to consider him less in that particular light, Dawn knew what he was thinking. Almost with bated breath, she waited to hear his answer. On that depended her future.

"I don't wish to influence you, but if you decide to stay, you will be everything here that Tarzan was on earth, the "Supplier" remarked, after almost a minute's silence. "And, if you decide to stay, at some time in the future we could arrange either for you to visit your family, or for them to come to see you."

"What about it, Dawn?" Bunduki asked.

"What do *you* think?" the girl countered, looking at his handsome if bruised face.

"We have Joar-Fane and At-Vee to consider," the blond giant pointed out. "With his ankle sprained, he can neither travel, hunt nor protect her adequately. So they'll be in danger until he's recovered. I'm going back to help him."

"Then so am I!" Dawn stated firmly and her right hand reached out to take hold of Bunduki's left.

When they looked behind them, the "Supplier"—whoever, or whatever, he might be—was dissolving into shimmering incandescence and disappeared in the same way that he had come.

"You will not see me again," came the voice from the fading glow. "Nor, while I can supply certain of your needs, can I render any physical or actual assistance. What happens now is entirely up to you."

"We wouldn't have it any other way," Bunduki declared and the girl at his side nodded her agreement.

Hand in hand, the blond giant and his beautiful companion walked onwards to their new life.

DAW⌐**sf**
BOOKS

Lin Carter's bestselling series!

☐ **UNDER THE GREEN STAR.** A marvel adventure in the grand tradition of Burroughs and Merritt. Book I.
(#UY1185—$1.25)

☐ **WHEN THE GREEN STAR CALLS.** Beyond Mars shines the beacon of exotic adventure. Book II. (#UY1267—$1.25)

☐ **BY THE LIGHT OF THE GREEN STAR.** Lost amid the giant trees, nothing daunted his search for his princess and her crown. Book III.
(#UY1268—$1.25)

☐ **AS THE GREEN STAR RISES.** Adrift on the uncharted sea of a nameless world, hope still burned bright. Book IV.
(#UY1156—$1.25)

☐ **IN THE GREEN STAR'S GLOW.** The grand climax of an adventure amid monsters and marvels of a far-off world. Book V.
(#UY1216—$1.25)

DAW BOOKS are represented by the publishers of Signet and Mentor Books, THE NEW AMERICAN LIBRARY, INC.

Presenting JOHN NORMAN in DAW editions . . .

☐ **TRIBESMEN OF GOR.** The tenth novel of Tarl Cabot takes him face to face with the Others' most dangerous plot—in the vast Tahari desert with its warring tribes, its bandit queen, and its treachery. (#UW1223—$1.50)

☐ **HUNTERS OF GOR.** The saga of Tarl Cabot on Earth's orbital counterpart reaches a climax as Tarl seeks his lost Talena among the outlaws and panther women of the wilderness. (#UW1102—$1.50)

☐ **MARAUDERS OF GOR.** The ninth novel of Tarl Cabot's adventures takes him to the northland of transplanted Vikings and into direct confrontation with the enemies of two worlds. (#UW1160—$1.50)

☐ **TIME SLAVE.** The creator of Gor brings back the days of the caveman in a vivid new novel of time travel and human destiny. (#UW1204—$1.50)

☐ **IMAGINATIVE SEX.** A study of the sexuality of male and female which leads to a new revelation of sensual liberation. Fifty-three imaginative situations are outlined, some of which are science-fictional in nature.
(#UJ1146—$1.95)

ALAN BURT AKERS—The first five great novels of Dray Prescot is The Delian Cycle:

☐ **TRANSIT TO SCORPIO.** The thrilling saga of Prescot of Antares among the wizards and nomads of Kregen. Book I.   (#UY1169—$1.25)

☐ **THE SUNS OF SCORPIO.** Among the colossus-builders and sea raiders of Kregen. Book II.   (#UY1191—$1.25)

☐ **WARRIOR OF SCORPIO.** Across the forbidden lands and the cities of madmen and fierce beasts. Book III.   (#UY1212—$1.25)

☐ **SWORDSHIPS OF SCORPIO.** Prescot allies himself with a pirate queen to rescue Vallia's traditional foes! Book IV.   (#UY1231—$1.25)

☐ **PRINCE OF SCORPIO.** Outlaw or crown prince—which was to be the fate of Prescot in the Empire of Vallia? Book V.   (#UY1251—$1.25)

DAW BOOKS are represented by the publishers of Signet and Mentor Books, THE NEW AMERICAN LIBRARY, INC.

THE NEW AMERICAN LIBRARY, INC.,
P.O. Box 999, Bergenfield, New Jersey 07621

Please send me the DAW BOOKS I have checked above. I am enclosing
$_____(check or money order—no currency or C.O.D.'s).
Please include the list price plus 25¢ a copy to cover mailing costs.

Name_____

Address_____

City_____State_____Zip Code_____
Please allow at least 3 weeks for delivery

ALAN BURT AKERS
Six terrific novels compose the second great series
of adventure of Dray Prescot: The Havilfar Cycle.

☐ **MANHOUNDS OF ANTARES.** Dray Prescot on the unknown continent of Havilfar seeks the secret of the air-
boats. Book VI. (#UY1124—$1.25)

☐ **ARENA OF ANTARES.** Prescot confronts strange beasts
and fiercer men on that enemy continent. Book VII.
(#UY1145—$1.25)

☐ **FLIERS OF ANTARES.** In the very heart of his enemies,
Prescot roots out the secrets of flying. Book VIII.
(#UY1165—$1.25)

☐ **BLADESMAN OF ANTARES.** King or slave? Savior or be-
trayer? Prescot confronts his choices. Book IX.
(#UY1188—$1.25)

☐ **AVENGER OF ANTARES.** Prescot must fight for his enemies in order to save his friends! Book X.
(#UY1208—$1.25)

☐ **ARMADA OF ANTARES.** All the forces of two continents
mass for the final showdown with Havilfar's ambitious
queen. Book XI. (#UY1227—$1.25)

**DAW BOOKS are represented by the publishers of Signet
and Mentor Books, THE NEW AMERICAN LIBRARY, INC.**
